I0520046

The Whistling Man 2

Rise of the Underworld

By

Will Savive

Del-Grande Publishing

Hackensack, New Jersey

Copyright © 2021 Will Savive/Del-Grande
Publishing

ISBN: 978-0-578-86923-0

ASIN: B08YN7PQ49

Author's Website:

https://willsavive.com/

The Whistling Man 2

Rise of the Underworld

Copyright © 2021 by Will Savive

To get all the latest news on horror movies & books, join:

https://www.facebook.com/dawhistlingman

ISBN-13: 978-0-578-86923-0
BISAC: Horror/Thriller

Printed in the United States of America

The Whistling Man 2

Rise of the Underworld

Chapter 1

December 22, 2019 Pavoso, Venezuela

Twenty-five maintenance workers (20 men & 5 women) are collecting their things for the trip home. It's been a long five days, particularly after the now-infamous incident that occurred there only a little over a month ago. Only days after, this same crew was sent in to clean up and retrieve the bodies. The military only conducted a brief investigation, about two days. The investigation was led by military officer, Renier Rodriguez, the Maestro Técnico Supervisor (Chief Warrant Officer) of the Venezuelan Army. Rumors flew around the country like leaves flying off of trees in the fall right from the beginning. It wasn't just the half-hearted investigation that raised the public's suspicions. Though, that didn't help any. The story gained international attention, even. The consensus all over the world, and the official story that people were fed, was that Laurie was responsible for the killings.

Laurie had died of gunshot wounds from incoming Soldiers, or at least that's what the world was told. It was an international mystery and no one knew what to make of it. But in Venezuela, however, everyone knew what had really happened. They were sure. It was The Whistling Man, *El Silbón*! And as for Laurie; she was missing. Her body never recovered. According to Venezuelan popular consensus, she was likely killed to shut her up.

The crew never stayed overnight. At a certain time, the crew would pack up and take a boat out of *Pavoso* and stay in a nearby town. They always made sure to leave Pavoso before nightfall. They would travel back in the morning and continue their work then. All five days would be the same routine. Up until now, no crew member had seen or encountered The Whistling Man. Having worked on the property for years, most of the crew was somewhat skeptical about the existence of The Whistling Man, but they still remained cautious. They worked in crews of five. No one ever went off on their own. Everyone must be accounted for at all times. It was the buddy system for watching each other's backs. There were several roll-calls throughout the day as well.

Most importantly, they had dogs! Plenty of them. Ten, to be exact. Five supervisors, not included in the twenty-five maintenance workers, were responsible for the dogs. One person from each crew was responsible for one dog. These dogs were highly trained. They would not run away, and they would protect the crew with their lives. The other five dogs were kept as reserves and for reinforcement purposes.

They met at the cabin for the first of the final two roll-calls. From there they walked in formations of fives on their way back to the dock. Five rows of workers moved east down *Main Road*. Pedro was always in the last row. He had gotten assigned to the unit with the three trouble-makers of the group. They called themselves "El Camarilla" ("The Clique"). Pedro was the outcast and was picked on frequently by the other three. Hector was the fourth member of that crew. He remained neutral. They left him alone because he did all of their dirty work and acquiesced to any of their demands amicably.

The weather is quite warm considering it is December. Most of the snow had begun melting. The air is cold enough to condense water vapor into droplets, but not cold enough to make it freeze. This caused an extremely thick fog that covered the entire town.

Pedro is wearing a navy-blue hoodie and brown cargo pants as he walks with the group to the dock. Pedro is walking a few steps ahead of the others, to their left, when he feels a pebble bounce off of his head. He turns around. Jorge, Marcel, and Pablo are all snickering. Hector has his head down. He raises his eyes, nervously, to meet Pedro's, and then he lowers them quickly. He wants no part of the absurdity. He tried to intervene once a while back and the clique's vitriol wound up focused on him. That was the first and last time he ever interfered in the clique's follies. Jorge, the leader of the clique, was usually the one who initiated any type of delinquency. He picked up another small pebble and lobbed it forward.

BING!

This one hit Pedro on his left shoulder. Pedro knew better than to challenge the clique. It would only make them more aggressive. He stayed silent, knowing that they would eventually get bored. As they passed Route 9, a horned owl sat on a branch in a nearby tree. He wore a menacing stare as he watched the crew walk by. As they walked further, the owl flew off in the direction of the old police station. Once they arrived at the dock the final roll-call began. Pedro, however, was getting antsy.

"I have to go take a piss real quick," he tells Hector. Pedro runs to the front of the police station where he has privacy.

"Where's he going?" Jorge says angrily, as he watches Pedro run away.

"He went to take a piss," said Hector.

"Make sure you sit down when you go, *Gilipollas (dumbass)*!" Pablo screams to Pedro. Jorge and Marcel chuckle.

Pedro unzips his pants and begins to pee. He lets out a sigh of relief, as his stomach slowly goes from uncomfortably swollen back to normal. About a dozen black crows are strangely circling above the police station; some making an eerie cawing sound. Pedro starts thinking about the clique taunting him. He hates them and wants so badly to get back at them. His concentration is broken, however, by a whistling-screaming sound that sounds far away. Pedro turns his waist, still peeing on the police station wall, and looks around. 'Was that the sound of The Whistling Man that [he] had been warned of?' he thought. 'Nah, can't be.' He zipped up his pants and turns around to go back to the group.

Standing there, as he turns, is the creature!

Pedro's face turns pale white. The creature puts his large hands on Pedro's head and twists it furiously, snapping his neck and killing him instantly. The creature takes off Pedro's pants and hoodie and then guts Pedro him. He puts one of his bones in a bloody sack. The creature walks slowly to the boat. He is wearing Pedro's clothes. His hood is covering his face. He keeps his head low as not to draw attention.

"Finally, you're back," Hector says. "I thought you were going to get in trouble." The figure remains silent. "Try to stay away from those guys," Hector warns. "They really got it out for you today." Hector and the creature both get checked in. The dogs are barking unusually loud as they are getting put into their cages for the boat ride home. Hector sees the clique over on the left talking to others, near the dogs. Hector makes a right. The creature follows him. They sit down and get ready for the half-hour-long voyage. But minutes later, the three members of the clique walk over and sit across from Hector and the creature.

"What's with that dirty bag?" Marcel asks the creature, who just keeps his head down.

"Are you deaf?" asks Jorge. "Marcel just asked you a question."

"I don't think he is feeling well, guys," says Hector. The creature coughs, and a bit of sticky bile drips to the ground.

"Damn!" Pablo exclaims in disgust. "Maybe we should have left him back there with El Silbón."

"Yeah, El Silbón," Jorge says, as he lets out a mocking laugh. "If I ever see El Silbón, I will gut him myself!" The creature clenches his fist in anger. Still, he must remain covert for at least a little while longer, until they get to shore, which is only a few more minutes.

The dogs bark frequently for the entire boat ride. They only take short breaks in between minutes of angry barking.

"Shut up you mangy mutts," shouts one of the supervisors, as he smacks one dog's cage. The boat makes the turn around the mountain where land can be seen. It's only minutes until the group arrives in the small town of *Guanarito*. As they approach the shore the dogs start barking louder and more frequently before.

"What the hell is wrong with those stupid dogs?" Pablo asks.

"Those stupid dogs might be the reason we are all still alive, Ese," Marcel retorts.

"Maybe they're hungry," Jorge suggests. "Maybe we should feed Pedro to them once the boat stops?"

"I don't know," says Pablo. "I don't think that will fill them up." Jorge and Marcel start laughing. The creature, however, does not. He clenched up his other fist this time. The boat is only inches from the shore. The creature raises his head, as the trouble makers are laughing at Pablo's last comment. He pulls down his hood and lets out a horrifying screeching sound. Jorge's face turns as white as a ghost as the monster stands aggressively to his feet and begins his furious attack!

The Whistling Man 2

Chapter 2

Caracas Psychiatric Hospital (Three days until Christmas)

Among the many disturbing characteristics of Venezuela's political and economic turmoil is the fact that their public health system has all but collapsed. There is a severe shortage of medications, and many of the good doctors have left the country. Nowhere is this more evident than seen in psychiatric facilities. Even in their finest facility, the *Caracas Psychiatric Hospital*; conditions have deteriorated significantly. Making matters worse, the political corruption in the country has even seeped into the mental health category. Several political prisoners and dissidents are being held in *Unit C* of the hospital. This is "the shadow unit," as they call it. Only those with the highest level of security in the hospital can enter this Unit. Aside from hospital staff, no one knows it even exists, except for a handful of high-ranking military and government officials.

A woman sits on the floor in the corner of her room. Her knees bent upwards; her arms resting on top of them; her hair, greasy, and covering her face. She appears heavily drugged. The room is rancid. The paint is peeling from the walls. The ceiling is rife with mold and water damage. The floor is wet in some areas and dirty everywhere. The smell is horrendous. The woman is ragged. She wears only a dirty hospital gown. A piece of paper on the wall tells of the schedule of the week's events:

Unit C Schedule as Follows:
Breakfast - 7:30 a.m.
Doctor Visit - 9 a.m.
Lunch - 11:30 a.m.
Individual Psychotherapy – 1:30 p.m.
Social Time: 3 p.m. – 5 p.m.
Dinner – 6 p.m. (in cell)
Lights Out 10 p.m.

A woman wearing a white tunic and a nurse's cap walks down the north-side hallway of Unit C. She arrives at a cell. Her nametag reads, 'Nurse Maria Gonzales.' She slides open the small sliding barn-door peephole on the metal door.

"Time for lunch, Ms. Orsted. Hustle up!" The woman on the floor looks up slowly. Her hair slides off of her face, exposing her features.

It's *Laurie Orsted*!

Laurie gathers herself and walks down to the mess hall, as they call it there. An eclectic group of individuals is gathered here. Most are what the government considers 'political prisoners,' because they have been vocal in their criticism of government leadership. Some others are 'the uncontrollables,' aptly named for the severely mentally ill that cannot control themselves. They have a tendency to freak out (not particularly known for violence, but vocally animated) on occasion without any provocation, and it appears as though it's almost unwittingly. A handful are the severely mentally ill who have shown a strong tendency for violence. This small group all wear muzzles when in with the general population. And then there is Laurie. Five-armed military guards are stationed at all of the large gatherings in Unit C.

Laurie stands in a long line waiting for food. When it's her turn a woman with a black hairnet slops a wet, gooey, green pile of food on her plate.

"Thanks," Laurie says sarcastically, "just what I was craving." The woman smiles sarcastically in return. Laurie walks by several rows of long cafeteria tables until she reaches an empty section. Just then, a patient stands up and throws his food plate across the room.

"I won't eat this shit anymore!" he screams. "I want a steak, medium-well with a baked potato and string beans, now!" He begins to slowly walk around to another table, screaming to others who are sitting quietly and eating. "Don't you want a steak or some chicken?" he shouts. Others start cheering him on. One man stands and screams, "Yeah, where is my fucking steak?"

"You see?" The original man says. "We need to band together. We are facing a great injustice here!" Two guards quickly descend upon the man. One guard hits him in the back of the head with the butt of his machine gun. The man falls like a sack of potatoes. By now, the crowd has gotten a bit rowdy. This act of aggression only further agitates them. The Soldier uses the butt of the gun again, hitting him several times in the ribs and legs. Along with this brutal display, other security guards point their guns at the loudest patients.

"Sit the fuck down or I will shoot you!" One guard firmly announces. Very quickly, this display of mutiny is shut down. Patients went right back to eating and silence was restored, like the battered and the bloodied patient was dragged out of the cafeteria by the two security guards. Each guard had one of the man's arms. His knees bent and his feet dragged on the ground as the guards carried his tattered body through the cafeteria doors. Jose and Mauricio, the two muscular orderlies quickly administered a shot of diazepam, which calms the patient within about sixty seconds. The orderlies then escort him, roughly, to *solitary*, while the security guards quickly get back inside the cafeteria to maintain order.

Moments after the incident, a male patient takes a seat across from Laurie.

"You're that woman from the Pavoso incident, right?"

"And you are?" Laurie asks.

"I'm Cassius Sanchez. I was second in command in the Venezuelan Army behind that prick, Renier Rodriguez."

"Really?" Laurie says. "So, what are you doing here?" Cassius chuckles.

"Haven't you heard? You can't have an opposing government view in this country."

"No, not really," Laurie retorts. "I don't know much about it here, actually. I doubt I will ever get used to it. You still haven't told me why you are in here, sir."

"I was accused of treason. They said that I was part of a military uprising in April. My lawyers were not even allowed to be present when I was brought before a judge. Basically, I'm accused of plotting against the government, because I voiced my concerns with certain human rights violations. The two previous administrations stacked the courts with judges who make no pretense of independence. It's all rigged. They will never let us out of here. Especially you."

"Me, why me?!" Laurie asks anxiously.

"Because you saw the elusive El Silbón! Did you really see him?"

"Well, I'm an American," Laurie proclaims. "They can't do this to me!"

"Oh, the news media said you were killed. No one is looking for you."

"They what!?" Laurie exclaims.

"Trust me, I heard all about it. I was there when Renier was discussing it. He said he was here the day you were brought in. Said he told Dr. Hernandez to keep you here indefinitely until they figured out what to do with you. Most likely you will be executed along with the rest of us."

"They, they can't do that," said Laurie, as a tear ran down her cheek.

"Oh, they are doing it. They are doing it to us all. Look around. The only way out of here is by death or escape. And there is a slim chance of escape. But the first thing you need to do is stop taking those pills they give you."

"How am I supposed to do that?" Laurie asked. "They watch everyone to be sure we take them."

"When it's in your mouth, slide it under your tongue. Then drink the water and make-believe you swallowed it." Laurie, still a bit woozy from the drugs given to her in the morning, shakes her head slightly in agreement.

Suddenly, a loud siren sounds, followed by an announcement over the loudspeaker (in the voice of nurse, Maria Gonzales).

"Lunchtime is over. Please proceed to station 12 and form a line."

"Remember what I told you," said Cassius, "Don't swallow the pills."

Everyone promptly stands up, disposes of the remaining food on their plates, and forms a line at the station 12 window. There are sixty patients in Unit C, far less than in the other two units. Today, fifty-six stand in line at station 12. Three are either sick or in solitary. The other, the man who caused a scene earlier, was taken to solitary confinement, where he will stay for at least a week. The Unit C population consists of 95% men and 5% women. Rape and murder of women in this unit are very common. Unlike the other two women in the unit, Laurie is a very high-profile inmate. Therefore, she is under closer observation in an isolated area of the unit.

The line moves quickly. Each patient approaches the window when it's their turn. The window is made of bullet-resistant plexiglass, with a small semi-circle hole at the bottom-middle where each patient is given a miniature dixie cup filled with water, one *Lorazepam* pill, and one *Haloperidol* pill. Each patient must put both pills in their mouth, flush them down with water, and then open their mouth's facing the administering nurse behind the Plexiglass. The nurse checks to be sure that both pills were ingested before giving the nod for the patient to head back to his or her cell.

Laurie walks up to the glass. Nurse Gonzales slides the two pills under the glass. Laurie scoops them up. The nurse slides the water under the glass. Laurie puts both pills in her mouth and grabs the cup of water. She puts the cup to her lips and jerks her head back quickly. She brings her head back down and opens her mouth.

The Nurse scans the inside of her mouth, looking for any signs that the pills have not been ingested. The nurse gives Laurie the nod to go. Cassius is right behind her waiting for his turn. Laurie turns and begins walking. She looks at Cassius and he back at her. Laurie opens her mouth slightly and shows him one of the pills, still in her mouth. She winks. Cassius smirks and walks up to the glass. Laurie takes the pills out of her mouth and puts them in her pocket.

As Laurie walks down the hall back to her cell, she is approached by a semi-balding, grey-haired, old White man.

"Hi, Mr. Peters," she says, "how are you? I didn't see you at lunch, again."

"Hello, my dear Laurie," he says with a heavy English accent. "I don't trust that Cassius character, or that Dr. Diaz. You should be careful what you say to them."

"I know, I have a funny feeling about them both," said Laurie. "But I don't want them to know that."

"Shall I walk you to your cell?"

"Sure," she says. The two continue down the winding hall. A one-armed guard is always close to Laurie. In this case, he is following about ten yards behind her. "That Cassius fellow just told me that the world thinks I'm dead and that I will never be let out of this hellhole unless I try to escape. I can't figure out why I'm here, but from what he said it makes sense."

"You are here because you witnessed something that the powers that be do not want people to know about," said Mr. Peters. "That he is right about. You need not faff about this. You need decisive action."

"But what do I do?" Laurie asks inquisitively.

"You needn't worry," he says. "Many forces are working in your favor. You need to be careful of Cassius and Dr. Diaz. They are both proper geezers. You must leave this place and give your friend, James, a call. He is the conduit between you and the information you need."

"How do you know James?" Laurie asked confusedly.

"Ah, ah, you mentioned him once before to me," said Mr. Peters, sounding a tiny bit flustered by the question.

"Oh, okay," said Laurie, a bit

confused still. They had conversed several times during her stay. Also, she had been drugged during most of their conversations. So, it was easy for her to assume that she had mentioned her best friend to Mr. Peter's at some point.

"Don't over-egg the pudding, dear," said Mr. Peters. "If you do not leave this place before Christmas, they will pop your clogs. You must wangle through the next day or two, appear zonked, and then be full of beans and leg it."

"Oh, well thanks," Laurie says sarcastically and confusedly. "You sound a bit like Dizzy with an English accent." Laurie chuckles softly.

"There are a lot of people counting on you, myself included. I must go now. Remember what I said!" Mr. Peters abruptly walks off.

"I don't even know what he just said," Laurie murmurs to herself, "let alone remember it." Laurie takes it with a grain of salt and walks into her cell.

She enters the room. The door closes and a loud metallic thud sounds as the door is locked behind her. The guard retreats once the nurse locks the door. Laurie spits the two pills into the toilet and flushes them. She is left for a few moments to her thoughts. She lays on her thin mattress, where she can feel the springs in her back and tries to rest her mind for a moment, lying on her back. Unmedicated, however, the traumas come to the forefront of her mind. Somehow, though, after a few minutes of struggling with her mind's unwitting recall, she is able to sleep.

****

Laurie awakens. She feels a calm come over her that she hasn't felt since she had arrived in Pavoso. She is drowsy, feeling half asleep even. She looks around then lays back down slowly. Just as she closes her eyes, a woman in a white gown says, "You can't stay here!" The audio is distorted. She opens her eyes brusquely. She sees the figure, whose opacity is evident.

"Who are you?" Laurie asks softly, barely able to get the words out.

"You must walk toward the 1st Ward after your session, 1st Ward!"

****

Laurie sits up, snappishly! Her eyes were now wide open. Her hair is wet from perspiration. She looks around. No one is there. '1st Ward?' she thinks. 'What was that about? It felt so real.'

Then, a brisk knock on her door just before it opens swiftly.

"Time for one-on-one," nurse Gonzales says. Laurie walks the hallway with a guard following behind her. Nurse Gonzales is leading the way. This is one of many sessions that Laurie has had with Dr. Diaz. She trusted him originally. But Laurie is a good judge of character. Dr. Diaz made the fatal mistake of underestimating her intelligence. One of Laurie's main gifts is that she can read people very quickly. Laurie does not trust him. To her, he is not working in her best interest. Especially after what Cassius had told her. She is starting to tie this all together. Moreover, she is soberer than she has ever been since she arrived at the facility. Although, she will continue to appear sedated outwardly for her own protection. During their first few meetings, Laurie had opened up to Dr. Diaz. She believed in giving the system a chance. And because what she was saying was the truth, and that she was a well-educated American; she believed that she would gain favor by telling the truth and articulating it well. However, getting the opposite result, she was now questioning everything.

"Welcome, again, Laurie," the doctor said.

"Hello, doctor. How have you been?" she asked.

"I'm good. And you?"

"I've had better days, but I am doing my best."

"Good," he said, "That's all you can do in this life." Laurie and the doctor both take their seats.

"So, tell me, Laurie. What's new?"

"Nothing much, doctor. I have been mostly having flashbacks of what happened, and trying to grieve properly and sort things out."

"Great," the doctor retorted. "And has Mr. Peters visited you lately?"

"Why do you always ask me about

Mr. Peters?" Laurie asked.

"Well, we have reason to believe that he seeks out those that are responsive to him and tries to manipulate them. He has been diagnosed as a compulsive liar."

"I just don't get that vibe from him," said Laurie. "He seems like a very nice man." Laurie was normally much more open with the doctor. But she had a much more guarded feeling this time. But she did not want him to sense this. "Basically, I just take what he says with a grain of salt. I don't give it much thought," she said.

"Interesting," Dr. Diaz responds, "normally you hold his word in such high regard."

"Well, he hasn't done much for me here, I am starting to realize," she said.

"I'm not feeling well, doctor. Can we cut this short and make up the time next time?"

"Sure, Laurie. I know you have been overwhelmed with stress lately. Get some rest and we will talk tomorrow. I know the guard is not back yet, as you were scheduled to be here longer, but I will write you a note and I am trusting that you will return to the nurse's station immediately for them to let you in to your cell."

"Yes, thank you, doctor. My head is spinning right now."

"Okay," he said graciously, "I will also give you a prescription for your headache."

"Thank you, doctor," she responded. Laurie took both scripts and began walking down the west hallway. She looked around discreetly, before darting, covertly, through the elevator hallway toward the 1st Ward. She had no clue what she was looking for. She just remembered the dream and the woman telling her to go there. She even thought to herself that this was a very risky endeavor—one that was most likely fruitless—but something inside of her was telling her to proceed. It was irresistible.

The hall was mostly dark. The first door as she entered the ward is the Doctor's conference room, which was brightly lit, with the door slightly open. She heard voices coming from the room. She slowed her pace and tip-toed to the edge of the doorway to get a better listen.

"I have given her the idea of escape," said one voice. Laurie peeked in and saw it was Cassius. "I think she will take the bait," he continued.

"Good," said Dr. Hernandez, "the hire-ups want a reason to terminate her, but they want it to look provoked. Someone in the American Embassy has been alerted to her presence here. And they will be putting pressure on us for her release. We need to have this done quickly."

"I just need a few more days to gain her trust," said Cassius.

"Okay," the doctor said, "but make it quick. Time is running out!" Just then, nurse Gonzales entered the room from through a door on the other side.

"I'm leaving now," she told Dr. Hernandez. "Do you need me to do anything else?"

"No, you are good," he said. "Has Daniela arrived yet?"

"Yes, she is getting changed," she answered.

"Good. Send her in here once you complete the shift change and you can go." Nurse Gonzales begins walking toward the door that Laurie is peeking in from. Laurie runs off. Nurse Gonzales hears a noise in the dark hallway. "Hello?" she says. "Who is there?" She looks around. After a few seconds, she shrugs it off and continues down the hallway. Laurie exits the janitor's closet, which is a few feet away from the doorway. A few doors down, Laurie hears fretful screams. She peeks in the room through the glass door and sees a man being treated by electroshock therapy. The man, in a straitjacket, screams from the torturous, high voltage electromagnetic pulses being sent through his body. He looks over at Laurie, as the two men in white lab coats have their backs to her. The two lock eyes. He stares at her as the next shockwave rocks his very foundation. He lets out a horrific scream, as he looks into Laurie's eyes, seemingly asking her for help. Laurie turns away in disgust. She cannot bear to watch any longer, and there is nothing she can do to help the man. The otherwise empathetic Laurie tapped into cognitive dissonance. She thought to herself, 'maybe he deserved what he was getting or maybe it will help him, ultimately.' She knew this was not the truth, but in order to help her move on from such an atrocity, she needed to quickly justify it and make peace before she could refocus on her own plight. She continues slowly ahead, creeping back to the nurse's station, with time to spare. She knows, however, that her situation has gone from bad to worse.

Chapter 3

Sifting Through the Wreckage

The boat in which the maintenance workers left Pavoso in was now motionless, stationed both in the water as well as being wedged into the land. Several Venezuelan police occupied the surrounding area. It looked as though the entire *Guanarito Police Department* was at the scene. Bodies are strewn in and around the small boat. Some are face down in the water, some are face-up, and some are in awkward positions. However, they all had one thing in common: they were all brutally murdered, all severely gutted, and all missing a bone. Anyone worth their salt could see that this was a massacre of epic proportions.

An army jeep races in and comes to an abrupt halt at the perimeter of the scene. The jeep is followed by an army truck filled with armed Soldiers dressed in camouflage army fatigues, who promptly jump from the back of the truck upon it stopping. Chief Warrant Officer, Renier Rodriguez, jumps out of the passenger side of the jeep before it even comes to a full stop. He is dressed in camouflage army fatigues, a red paratrooper's beret (with a silvered colored badge off to the left side of his head), and combat boots.

"Chief," the lieutenant says greeting him, as he performs a rigid salute. Chief Rodriguez is a very well-known figure in Venezuela, a celebrity of sorts, in fact. He is known for his methodical speech, deep, intimidating voice, taciturn communicative style, and morose attitude. A smile never crosses his face, at least not one that anyone could testify to witnessing.

"What the hell happened here?" the Chief askes adamantly. "Looks like a God-damned war zone!"

"According to that gentleman over there (the lieutenant points to Hector), The Whistling Man did this. You believe this bullshit, someone claiming such nonsense?"

Hector is sitting on a big rock, clutching both ends of the blanket that is covering him. He is visibly shaken.

"And who the hell is he?" asked the Chief.

"He is part of the maintenance crew," the lieutenant responds. "He is the only person still alive. We believe he is involved somehow." Hector's face is battered and bruised from police interrogation. "We tried, but couldn't get anything out of him."

"The rest are deceased?" asked Chief Rodriguez.

"Yeah," said the lieutenant. "we collected all of the IDs except for three. We are still awaiting the IDs of the two victims in the water." Chief Rodriguez looks over and sees one of the officers fishing a body out with a long metal pole with a hook on it, and another officer doing the same, close by, with the other body. "This guy over here (the lieutenant points to a mangled body on the ground) is the only one who has been searched so far and does not have any ID. Good old Hector, over there, says this guy is, or was, a man named Jorge."

"Well, how the hell can he tell?"

asked Chief Rodriguez. "It looks like someone stomped a mudhole in his head."

"Sure does," said the lieutenant.

Chief Rodriguez walks over to Hector, accompanied by two armed Soldiers.

"Which way did he go?" Chief Rodriguez asks firmly and without hesitation. Hector points straight into the mainland, away from the water. "What is he wearing?" he asks.

"I thought he was Pedro," said Hector in a trembling voice. "While still in Pavoso, Pedro went to take a piss. El Silbón came back wearing Pedro's clothes: a navy-blue hoodie and cargo pants." Chief Rodriguez turns to the Soldier on his right.

"Call Pavoso P.D.," he said. "Tell them there is another victim there. And tell them they're going to need a new cleaning crew."

Chief Rodriguez gives a nod to the two Soldiers, who promptly and forcefully take Hector into custody.

"Hey wait a minute," Hector shouts, as they drag him away. "I didn't do anything." Chief Rodriguez walks back over to the lieutenant.

"I'm taking this Hector character into

custody to question him. I don't want anyone finding out about this, you hear me?" he proclaimed resolutely. "Not a soul!"

"Sure thing, Chief, you can count on me."

"And get this cleaned up fast! A big storm is coming in!" the Chief explained.

"I know," said the lieutenant. "We are supposed to get 70 mph winds and heavy rain." Just then, something fell from the sky and landed on the Chief's left shoulder.

PLOP!

The Chief used his right hand to wipe off the splattering with his leather gloves. He put his hand to his nose and took a whiff. He grimaced.

"God, dammed bird shit!" he announced. He looked up and saw about a dozen crows circling above. "As you were lieutenant."

Just as quickly as they had arrived, Chief Rodriguez and his Soldiers sped off with Hector in custody.

The Powers Within

Laurie sat quietly back in her cell. She pondered the day's events, and what she had been told by both Cassius and Mr. Peters. These revelations were the first sense of clarity she had felt since she had arrived. She was always a confident person and relied on her instinct. However, the lack of information, the drugs, and the isolation had distorted her thinking. She was now overwhelmed with lucid thoughts from all of the information she had received. And, without the drugs to make her complacent and submissive, she was beginning to feel more like herself. She is a fighter. She is logical. She is intelligent. She is smart. She is practical. All of these qualities were rushing back to her at the same time. But, like a USB flash drive downloading a large amount of information would take some time. And—only just recently becoming lucid—it would take some time for her to catch up with the plethora of information thrown at her over many weeks.

Sitting on her bed, motionless, legs

again bent, arms resting on them, head down; Laurie hears a slight chitter that breaks the eerie silence. She raises her head and sees a tiny mouse squeeze in her cell through a tiny crack where the wall meets the floor. Because Laurie is motionless, the mouse does not notice her at first. Laurie stays motionless, happy to see any type of life form at this point. The mouse looks up and freezes once he identifies the large human sitting on the bed. He is stunned. Laurie notices a large, semi-round brown spot on top of the otherwise grey mouse's head. The mouse pauses, remaining frightfully still. He is not sure if the human has seen him or not.

"It's okay, Mousey," Laurie says in a non-threatening tone. The mouse hears the sound and begins running away. "Wait, Mousey!" she shouts; but not with her mouth, rather with her mind. The mouse halts. The mouse turns and walks over to the foot of the bed. Now, it's Laurie that is stunned. 'Did I just do that?' she thought. 'No, that's not possible.' She then experiments a bit. Out loud, she says, "Climb up on my bed." But the mouse only looks at her as if he does not understand. "Come on," she says. Still, nothing. Then she closes her eyes and concentrates. She clears her mind. She does not say a word. Instead, she uses her inner voice. She feels a weird feeling, like a tingling, as she gains focus. "On the bed," she says in her mind. She opens one eye, leaving the other closed. A hail-Mary, of sorts. The mouse is on the bed and puts his two front legs on her left thigh, timidly.

Laurie is stunned! 'Did I just do that?' she wonders.

With a bit more confidence, Laurie opens both eyes and says in her inside voice, 'Spin around.' The mouse surprisingly complies. He spins once and then looks up at her as if awaiting further instructions. She pushes her chin forward while thinking the phrase, 'Mousy (as she had aptly named him), run over to that wall then back to my feet.' Low and behold, the mouse leaps from the bed and runs to the wall and back. Laurie was flabbergasted. She still needed more proof, though. 'Go get three more mice and bring them to me,' she said, again in her mind's voice. The mouse ran off through the hole in which he arrived. Minutes went by; then minutes. 'Was I hallucinating?' she thought.

After a while, she chalked it up to her strange circumstance. Her new high, which was a rarity in this place, now sank to an all-time low. She put her head on her pillow, lying on her back, and stretching out. She stared at the ceiling, as she always did. This time, however, it looked a bit different. The sobering reality of where she was and what she had become was all too real. For the first time in this place, she had clarity, and she questioned whether it was a blessing or a curse.

She cursed Cassius. 'I should have taken those pills,' she thought, as she began having withdrawals. No one needs to be sober in this place. Even the strongest person cracks in these types of environments. 'Especially the strongest,' she thought.

"Chitter, chitter, chitter," is all she heard next.

She thought that she was imagining it at first. She turned her head on the pillow and saw Mousey with three other mice.

They were all looking up at her as if she were their new ruler. She turned her head back to the ceiling for a moment. She had not processed her thoughts just yet.

Bam!

Her head swung back to the mice with great force. They were still there, in the same position. She swung her feet around and sat up on the bed. She stared at them for a moment, making sure they were real. 'Even if this is a dream,' she thought, 'it's still awesome.'

Suddenly, she heard the sound of keys jangling. Moments later, the door swung open.

"Hey, how are you holding up?" the woman entering asked.

"Daniela?" asked Laurie, whose eyes were squinting from the excessive light. "Is that you?" The mice scatted quickly.

"Yes, my dear. I just changed shifts with Maria. Come closer, I need a word with you." Laurie stands and walks over to the peephole in the door.

"I hope it's good news," Laurie said. "I can't bear more bad news."

"Listen carefully!" Nurse Daniela

Perez announced to her firmly (whispering, as not to be overheard by the guard). "A man by the name of Hector just arrived here in Unit C, on the southside. He was part of the clean-up crew over in Pavoso. His whole group was massacred on the boat trip from Pavoso to Guanarito. He claims that '*El Silbón*' killed everyone but him and fled toward the border."

"When did this happen?" Laurie asked.

"This afternoon," nurse Daniela remarked.

"I need to speak with him immediately, Daniela, please," Laurie begged.

"Yes, I will arrange it," the nurse said, "but he is under very tight security, even tighter than you right now. We will need to wait until late at night when everyone is sleeping."

"What about the guard?" Laurie asked.

"I will take care of that. Just be ready," she said just above a whisper before exiting the cell.

Chapter 4

Wrong Place, Wrong Time

It's midnight in Venezuela, twenty-four hours until Christmas. In Venezuela, they celebrate Christmas on December 24th. Not many hours left until Santo Clós (Santa Claus) comes down the chimney. And the two children [7 & 10] living with their mother and father (in the beautiful two-story house just outside of Caracas, Venezuela) are ecstatic. Their excitement boils over as their parents tuck them in for the night. It's doubtful that they will get much sleep the following night. The mother is softly singing them the old Venezuelan lullaby, *Duerme Negrito*. Outside, there are a bunch of crows circling high above the house in silence.

The mother exits the room quietly. She closes the door ever so delicately. She waits for a second to see if she hears movement, but there is none. She walks downstairs ebulliently, as she was looking forward to spending some alone time with her husband.

"Are they asleep?" he asks, as she is walking down the stairs.

"They are out cold," she replies.

"We are finally alone," he says, as he pulls her close and gives her a romantic kiss. A bottle of wine, two wine glasses, and some cheese and crackers are set on the living room table.

"Aww," she said romantically, "you prepared that for us?"

"Well, it is your birthday today," he says. "Here." He hands her a birthday card and a small wrapped gift.

"You didn't have to do that, hun."

"Just open it." She unwrapped the gift and opened the small box.

"Oh My," she says with a sigh. "How

did you know?"

"I heard you on the phone the other day with your mother saying you saw this beautiful ankle bracelet. So, I called your mother and asked her where you saw it."

"That is so sweet!" she cried.

"I have dinner prepared as well," he announced. "Just let me take out the garbage first and then we can eat and you can open the card."

"Sounds like a plan," she answered. The man went into the kitchen and grabbed two full garbage bags that he had already tied and prepared for disposal.

He walked out the front door and around to the back of the house and placed both bags in the trashcan. It was very quiet out. That was until a screaming whistle sounded out. It sounded far away, but close enough to send a shiver up the man's spine. He walked back into the house and into the living room, where his wife was pouring wine for the both of them. She had also turned on some romantic Spanish music while he was outside.

"Did you hear that?" he asked.

"Hear what?" she replied.

"I don't know," he said disconcertedly. "It sounded like someone was screaming."

"I know I'll be screaming shortly," she teased. That comment was enough to make him forget what he had heard. Suddenly, a blur appeared to have darted from the front door past the living room area headed toward the kitchen.

"Did you see that?" the wife asked concern.

"I see something," the man said flirtatiously, as he eyed his wife.

"No, I'm serious," she said. "It looked like something just ran down the hall toward the kitchen, like a ghost or something. It was fast."

"You probably just imagined it," he said, as he walked to check the front door.

It was open!

"That's strange," he said. "The front door is open."

"Did you not close it when you came back in?" she asked.

"No, I'm sure I closed it," he said while scratching his head. Just then they hear a loud crashing sound coming from the basement.

"What the...?" he said.

"That was from the basement," she shouted.

"I know!" He replied firmly. "I will go check it out. Stay here." He grabbed a pointy brass poker tool from the fireplace. He walked from the living room into the hallway, where he was facing the side of the staircase. He made a left and headed into the kitchen.

"The basement door is open," he said. "I think an animal, like a cat or something, ran in. I will be right back."

"Be careful, hun!" she urged.

The stairs creaked as he slowly walked down with his flashlight on.

"Is anyone there?" he yelled. "I'm armed." No one answered, so he continued down the stairs. He is a pretty big man, about 6 foot, weighing 240 pounds. Still, he had no firearm weapon in the home, and 'if there was an intruder,' he thought, 'and the intruder had a gun he would be at an extreme disadvantage.' As he reached the bottom of the stairs, he flipped the switch on the wall up. Yet, the light did not go on.

He looked over at where the bulb was supposed to be screwed in on the ceiling, about ten feet to the left of the bottom of the staircase. However, the bulb was missing. "What?" he shouted. "I just replaced that bulb the other day. She must have unscrewed it. I told her to ask me before touching things. Okay, okay, calm down, it's her birthday. Don't go starting anything." He walked a little further into the basement, shining the light around. "Here kitty, kitty. Come on out. I won't hurt you." He scanned high and low but saw nothing. "Oh well," he said. He turned back around and headed toward the stairs. Out of the shadows, just in front of the stairs; the creature stepped forward with his head down and a hoodie covering his face.

"Who the fuck are you?" he asked firmly. He raised the brass poker into combat position. The creature then raised his head while pulling back his hood.

"ROAR!"

The creature exposed his deadly sharp teeth. Before the man could even get out a word, much less blink, the creature had closed the fifteen-foot distance between them in a millisecond. It appeared as though he had moved a great distance, instantaneously, without even taking a step. The man went to swing the poker, but the creature grabbed it before it moved an inch. He ripped it out of the man's hand and shoved it into his stomach.

Squelch!

It went through his belly and out his back. The man groaned and gasped. He lifted him off of the ground with the poker handle. Blood poured out of the man's mouth and nose, as he shook violently before going limp. The man fell to the ground, lifeless, with a thud, with the poker still impaling him.

The woman was drinking wine and dancing to the music. The music was loud enough that she didn't hear the commotion. She stopped brusquely and looked toward the hallway. "What's taking him so long?" she said. She put her wine glass on the coffee table and walked into the kitchen. "Hun?" she shouted. "Hun, it's my birthday and I wanna celebrate. Come on." After a few more seconds of silence, she had, had enough. "Oh, okay, so we are doing this? You are gonna mess with me now and try to scare me? I'm not scared. I'm coming down there!" She walked down the stairs with no fear. She was sure her husband was trying to scare her.

She reached the bottom of the stairs and saw that the switch to the light was in the upright position. 'hmm,' she thought. "Okay, this isn't funny. I don't have a flashlight." She paused for a moment. "You are really going to do this on my birthday?" she shouted. "Okay, I'm gonna go back upstairs now and lock the door. Let's see how funny it is then." Just as she began turning to go back up the stairs, she saw a lit flashlight on the ground to the left of the stairs and about 15 feet away. The darkness and clutter in the basement made it hard for her to see much, but she did see a slight glimmer from the light. "Hun?" she called out. She walked a few more feet toward the light. She saw an image, but she couldn't make out what it was. The flashlight was on, but it was dim. She got closer and bent down to pick up the flashlight. She rose slowly with the flashlight in hand. As soon as she stood up straight, she saw dangling feet. She aimed the flashlight a bit higher and saw her husband hanging from a rope that was tied to the eight-foot ceiling. He had been gutted; the inside of his stomach was completely exposed. She let out a dreadful scream and dropped the flashlight. Tears immediately streamed from her eyes. "No!" she screamed, frozen from shock and terror, as she began breathing heavily and whimpering. She heard footsteps approaching quickly to her left. She turned. The beast shoved the brass poker through her throat and out the back of her neck. Both her eyes and mouth were wide open with terror. He let go of the poker and she fell to the floor like a sack of beans.

The creature grabbed his full bag of bones. He hid them under the loose wooden floorboard. A few moments later the two children came running downstairs. They had heard the music playing. They walked through the house looking for their parents. First the living room; then the kitchen. "Mama?" they cried. "Daddy?" they shouted. They saw the door to the basement ajar. They both walked downstairs, terrified. They saw both their mother and father dead, gutted, and a bone missing from each. The creature had left minutes before the children had come downstairs.

Stow Away

A great horned owl flew across the sky. Just minutes away from the house where the creature had massacred a father and mother and left two traumatized children scarred for life. The owl flew toward Caracas. Forty miles per hour he flew until he got to Caracas International Airport. *Flight 157* had already been boarded and was about to take off. It was headed to Mexico City. The baggage handlers were just loading up some final items. The owl quickly flies into the luggage shoot of the plane while the baggage handlers are not looking. He hides behind a few bags. The plane takes off not long after. The owl has successfully, covertly hitched a ride on an airplane to Mexico City.

Chapter 5

Nurse in Chaining

It's midnight in Caracas (December 24th) and way past lights out at the psychiatric hospital. However, that never stopped some of the patients from causing a ruckus throughout the night. Unit C is no different, maybe even worse, in fact. Random howls, screams, cackles, and vulgar protests can be heard on any given night. And all night, for that matter.

A tropical storm had just hit the area. Wind gusts up to 73 mph knocked down trees and power lines. Rain of 2.5 inches pours over a radius of many miles, resulting in flash flooding of small streams, creeks, and rivers. Visibility has become limited. The power in the hospital suddenly goes out. The backup generators kick in immediately, but only power certain sections. All staircases remain lit. Most of Unit C is in darkness. Only the nurse's station remains illuminated. On the second floor, a little less than half of the floor is lit. On the first floor, everything is lit, with the exclusion of the entire first-floor ward. Also, on the first floor, some of the offices south of the *Patient Walkway* are experiencing outages. Most video cameras are also not active.

Laurie sits on her bed, unaware of the storm, praying for the return of nurse Daniela. She sits in the dark, regardless. A million thoughts run through her head. The litany of possible outcomes stemming from the impending escape brings mostly feelings of extreme anxiety. The only thought she had about the possibility of being outside the facility is getting in contact with her best friend, James Johnson. She knew if there was anyone she could count on, it is him. Moreover, she knew that he was worried about her. She hasn't spoken to anyone since she had left for Pavoso. And finding out that the world has been told she was dead only infuriated her. When she opens her eyes, she sees only darkness.

Just then she hears talking outside her door.

"A patient escaped!" the woman cried frantically. "He just ran into the mess hall and is screaming and demanding food." The guard rushes off while getting on his two-way radio to call for backup. The keys jangled for a few seconds before the door swings open.

It's Daniela!

She swiftly swung the large duffle bag to the ground that she had been carrying over her shoulder. She unzipped the bag and pulled out a white nurse's outfit with a hat to match.

"Hurry, put this on!" she said with urgency. Daniela laid the outfit out on the bed. Without hesitation, Laurie began stripping.

"Give me your clothes." Daniela took each article of Laurie's clothing and stuffed them one by one into the empty duffle bag.

"Hurry!" Daniela urges anxiously.

"They will be back any second if no

one is in the mess hall," said Laurie, as she raced to get the nurse's outfit on.

"Yeah," Daniela responded, "that's why I let out one of the crazies and told him there was food in there for him. He always complains that he is hungry, so." Both women let out a laugh.

"We need to pass by the mess hall to reach Hector as well as the staircase that leads out of here," Daniela explained. "So, we need to be ready to interact with the guards. Just keep your head low and let me do all the talking."

"Ah, yeah, I'm not gonna say a word," Laurie uttered.

"Someone must be looking out for you," said Daniela. "This timely power outage may just save us both." Laurie finishes getting dressed. "You clean up nice," Daniela said. "Let's go!" Daniela peeks her head out of the cell. When she sees that the coast is clear she walks quickly down the 2nd ward hallway. Laurie follows right next to her. Laurie is surprised to hear how many patients are not only still awake, but talking to themselves and saying very creepy things, no less. Daniela is carrying the large duffle bag, with the strap over her shoulder. They come to the end of the 2nd ward. They angle right just a bit past the lit nurse's station. Daniela drops the bag behind the nurse's desk. They see three guards apprehending the patient who had entered the cafeteria area. The patient is putting up a good fight, even though he is outnumbered.

"This way, hurry," Daniela says. They both make a right and walk down the large hallway, which quickly turns into the 3rd ward. They were only a few steps in when they heard a loud screaming voice,

"The Devil is here!"

The slow, deep rumble in his voice is spine-chilling. Laurie looks to her left and sees a man who appears to be wearing a white straight-jacket. He was looking through the small sliding barn-door peephole. He is looking at her intently. "He is going to get you, you know?!"

"Pay him no mind," said Daniela. "That's Mister Morales. He has been diagnosed with just about every mental disorder you can think of." Mr. Morales takes a few steps back then runs forward as fast as he can.

THUD!

He runs right into the door. Laurie flinches as his body violently crashes into the metal door. He grunts, and then repeats. Daniela closes his peephole. Still, he keeps ramming into the door as they walk off.

"Hector's cell is the last cell on the left," said Daniela. "You go talk to him and I'll keep lookout." Laurie walks forward, anxious as to what she will uncover. She comes upon the last cell on the left. She slides the peephole open. There sits Hector. He had been battered and beaten since he had been taken away by Chief Renier Rodriguez and his crew. He is badly bruised, slumped over, and holding his rib area.

"Hector?" Laurie asks compassionately.

"Who is that?" he asks, as he lifts his head up, but can barely see because of the beating he took.

"It's Laurie Orsted. The Whistling Man killed my three friends."

"Oh yes," said Hector, "You are very well known." He gasps from the pain.

"Did you really see him?" Laurie asked.

"Not only did I see him, but I watched him massacre my whole group, which included three of my cousins and many of my friends."

"I'm so sorry," Laurie says. "Why did he leave you alive, though?"

"I don't know. I've been thinking of that myself. Maybe to have a witness. I think he wants people to know he is alive. He likes the fear he commands."

"Who brought you here?" Laurie asked.

"Chief Renier Rodriguez," said Hector.

"Who is that?" she asked.

"He is the head of the Venezuelan Army and the second most powerful person in the country next to the President. I'm assuming you're here as well because of him. They don't want anyone to know for sure that El Silbón still lives. It would send the country into a panic." Laurie remembers back to when she awoke on the gurney the first time that she realized she was in a hospital. There, stood Dizzy, Dr. Hernandez, and a military officer.

"Oh shit," she said, "he was here talking to the doctor when I first arrived. He was wearing a red beret."

"Oh yes," said Hector, "that's him!"

"I will get you out of here," Laurie says. "Just give me some time."

"Much appreciated ma'am, but with all due respect, you are in here with me."

"I know," said Laurie, "Just be patient and don't tell anyone we spoke." Hector moved his head up and down slowly, looking as if it pained him to move at all. With that, Laurie walked off.

Now or Never

Laurie walks slowly back toward the nurse's station. Daniela is standing inside the large, round desk. She is trying to act inconspicuously, as if she is occupied with work. The guards have left the area. They are busy subduing the escaped patient. The two orderlies are administering medication to the patient in his cell. They intravenously give him Lorazepam, which increases the patient's risk of raspatory depression, but is fast-acting. They also combine that, intravenously, with Haloperidol, which by itself could lead to cardiac arrhythmias, aside from other negative effects. Moreover, Haloperidol is no longer licensed for intravenous use. But this hospital has never been one to follow the letter of the law. Regardless, it subdues the patient very quickly.

"Daniela, is there a chance I can stop by Mr. Peters' cell quickly to say goodbye?"

"Mr. who?" Daniela said confusedly.

"Mr. Peters, the old English gentleman who speaks with a heavy English accent," said Laurie. "He has been here for a long time, he said."

"Sweety, there is no Mr. Peters in Unit C or anywhere else in this hospital," Daniela said resolutely.

"But I talk to him almost every day," Laurie retorted. "He is in the 1st ward. I'm sure of it."

"Laurie, I assure you, there is no Mr. Peters here. And there is certainly no one in Unit C that speaks with an English accent."

"Huh?" Laurie said. She zoned out for a moment, remembering their last few conversations. Daniela grabs Laurie's arm.

"The guards will be back any second," Daniela warns. "We have to go; it's now or never."

"What about the video cameras?" Laurie asks. "Won't you be spotted?"

"There are only a few cameras that work with the backup generator," says Daniela. "I know the ones that don't work. Just follow me." They walk down the west hallway and make a sharp right just before entering the 1st ward. This small hallway leads to the staircase. Daniela uses her key to open the door to the staircase, as every exit in the building requires a key. They run down the stairs and come to a door which reads "2nd floor." Just as they pass that door, a security guard opens it. Daniela is ahead and just out of sight. Laurie, however, can still be seen.

"Hey!" he screams at Laurie. Instinctively, she stops momentarily and turns. Her eyes widen as she notices the guard. "Who are you?" he shouts aggressively. Daniela stops also. A rush of adrenaline runs through both women's veins. Daniela's career and freedom are now in jeopardy.

"Come on!" Daniela says just above a whisper. The two turn and head furiously for the 1ˢᵗ floor. The guard leans back into the 2ⁿᵈ floor hallway and screams to the other security guard he was just speaking to minutes earlier.

"Hey, we have an escapee, this way!" Both men immediately give chase. The two ladies reach the 1ˢᵗ floor entrance. Daniela also needs a key to exit the staircase. Both women are out of breath and breathing heavily. Daniela shuffles anxiously through her enormous set of keys, looking for the right one for this door.

"Hurry!" Laurie says quietly.

"I'm trying," said Daniela.

The fast-pouncing feet of the two security guards can be heard, and they are approaching quickly. The guard furthest behind radios the others.

"We have a patient from Unit C on the loose headed for the 1ˢᵗ floor. She is headed down the northern staircase!" Guards from every floor drop what they are doing to respond to the emergency.

Someone sounds the alarm! Daniela grabs a key. "Got it!" she says excitedly. The lead guard rounds the stairs and sees Laurie exiting onto the 1st floor. The door is halfway closed. He high-tails it to the door in an attempt to catch it before it shuts. Just as his hand reaches the door handle, the door shuts.

Click!

By now, the other guard had reached the door. They, too, needed a key for entry to the 1st floor. The lead guard scrambled through his keys anxiously, as Daniela did before him, to find the 1st floor north staircase key. Daniela and Laurie raced down the hallway and made a left-down *Patient Walkway* hallway, where they both hear some commotion coming from the only ward on the 1st floor, which is behind them. And the sounds are getting closer.

Daniela stops abruptly.

"Listen carefully," she says. "Go ahead of me. Go straight down this hallway. Before you reach the *Emergency Department*, make a left and exit through the *Employee Entrance*. Here is the key to exit."

"But what about..."

"Just go!" Daniela screams as she

hands her the key and pushes Laurie forward before Laurie can finish her statement. As Laurie runs with all her might, Daniela bangs her head against the brick wall, hard. Her eyelids flicker. She stumbles. She almost falls. She quickly regains composure and bends forwards, with blood now oozing from her head. She puts her hands on her knees. Three security guards come running from the 1st ward down *Patient Walkway*.

"She went that way," Daniela said, pointing to the hallway that intersects *Patient Walkway* and *Public Walkway* hallways. Both of these *Walkways* run parallel to one another. Two of the guards race down the intersecting hallway and make a right at *Public Walkway* hallway. That hallway leads to the front door of the hospital. The other guard stays behind to tend to Daniela.

"Are you okay?" the guard asked Daniela. "What happened?"

"She hit me with something, I don't know with what," Daniela said, groggy. She was woozy and sounded out of it. "She took my keys!"

"Okay, sit down here," he said, as he helped her to the ground. By now, her head had swelled and a big knot appeared and was turning black and blue.

Meanwhile, Daniela had sent Laurie in the opposite direction that she had sent the guards. Laurie opened the door labeled, *Employee Entrance*, and ran forward. A red 2019, Audi SQ7 SUV was parked sideways. The darkly tinted passenger side window slowly rolls down.

"Get in!" the man screamed.

"Dizzy?" Laurie exclaimed. "What the hell are you doing here?" she asked angrily. The last time she had seen him he was buddying up with Chief Rodriguez.

"Just get in, we don't have time!"

"I'm not going anywhere with you," said Laurie. "For all I know, you are the reason I'm in here."

"You're as lost as last year's Easter egg, darlin, now get in the car! Daniela told me to meet you here."

"Daniela?" Laurie said confusedly. Just then, one security guard bursts through the door.

"Hey!" he screams, as he unholsters

his gun.

"Oh, Chantilly Lace," Dizzy screams, "I'm fixin' to go; now get in!" he opens the door. Laurie jumps in quickly. Dizzy peels off.

BANG, BANG, BANG!

The shots ricochet off Dizzy's truck, as he skids out and makes a right down *Ambulance Way*, at the far-right end of the hospital.

"You might wanna buckle up, there, little lady," said Dizzy, driving at a high speed. "It's about to get as messy as a restroom at the end of Taco Tuesday up in here." Laurie buckles up, as Dizzy makes a hard left at the front of the hospital, with tires screeching. Two entrances down is the main entrance to the hospital. They had exited via the emergency entrance, which was the entrance to the emergency room. The guards out front spot the SUV skidding onto the road. One of the guards gets on his CB Radio.

"They are headed east down *Chavez Road*," he reports.

Chapter 6

Turbulence

"Ladies and gentlemen," the pilot announced, "please fasten your seat belts and prepare for landing." *Flight 157* was nearing the runway in Mexico City. It was a smooth flight and the overall consensus was jubilance. The stewardesses walked around with smiles making sure that all passengers had fastened their seat belts. Some commotion began stirring in the back of the plane, however. A few screams from the back rows grew louder and louder. One male passenger, in-seat A3 near the front of the plane, looked back and saw a few people screaming and waving their arms around. He laughed at first. Awkwardly, of course. The scene was so surreal that it was like having an out-of-body experience. Yet, a few seconds later he saw an owl flying around the heads of the passengers in the back.

Row by row, the owl terrorized passengers as it advanced, clawing at people's faces and heads. As it moved further toward the man in seat A3, he saw it a little clearer. By now, the number of screaming people had doubled. And the man gets a glimpse of the talon of the owl ripping out a man's eyeball. His nervous laughter quickly turned to horror. The owl hovered and struck randomly and fiercely. People began to dislodge from their seat belts and run frantically in the aisles, away from the trapped predator. Some people who were recently sleeping were awoken by a sharp talon to their sculls, unaware of why they were bleeding profusely.

One of the stewardesses ran to the cockpit and banged aggressively on the door. One of the pilots opened it.

"A killer owl is loose on the plane!" she screamed. The pilot, hearing complete panic, walked forward and pulled back the curtain. The owl flew furiously, some 30 mph, right past the pilot and into the cockpit. He quickly transformed into the beastly creature and closed the cockpit door. The captain, who was attending to the flight of the plane, turned, and to his dismay; he saw the fearsome creature salivating. The creature grabbed his head and began banging it sadistically and violently against the dashboard of the plane. One, two, three, four, etc., until the pilot's head caved in.

One stewardess banged on the door several times.

"Captain, are you okay?" she screamed. She continued banging but heard nothing. She waited, but there was complete silence. The other pilot walked over to her.

"What is going on?" he asked. She turned and faced him.

"I don't know, sir. The captain is not answering." The door swung halfway open and a large claw-like hand reached out and grabbed the stewardess from behind and pulled her into the cockpit. The door closed just as soon as it had opened. The co-pilot stood in shock. 'Was that the pilot who just pulled her in?' he thought. He walked slowly toward the door. He listened for any sounds but heard nothing. He crept closer and closer. His trepidation increased significantly with every step forward.

The plane then swerves to the right, dramatically. Most of the passengers let out dreaded screams, as they lost their footing. Some were thrown into other objects, like seats and the side of the plane. Some were thrown into others. The pilot outside the cockpit gets pushed to his right harshly and hits his head on a metal shelf. He falls to the ground. He quickly gathers himself and stands to his feet. He puts his right hand on his head and looks at it. His hand has blood on it. Suddenly, the cockpit door opens. The pilot is standing face to face with the awe-inspiring human predator. His shock does not afford him the benefit of movement. The creature holds up the throttle handle with the two steel rods on the end of it as if he had somehow ripped it cleanly from its setting. The twisted steel at the end of each protruding rod was mind-boggling if you knew the instrument well. The pilot looks at it as if mesmerized. In one swift motion, the creature jabs the throttle at his head, causing each side of the steel rods to go through both of the co-pilot's eyes.

The monster casually walks through the curtain, naked. Frightful screams fill the cabin. He stands there for a few seconds, looking at them menacingly. Then it appears as if he smirks, sadistically. The people look at him with confusion and panic. He then turns toward the door of the plane and charges it. He shoulder-blocks the door off its hinges, sending himself and the door flying into space. The plane's air pressure causes the plane to go into an irreversible dive toward the ground. With no one to pilot the plane, death to all is imminent.

The creature falls through the air like a skydiver. He then turns back into the owl and gracefully coasts through the air. He watches calmly and contently, as the plane slams into buildings in downtown Mexico City, causing a horrific explosion that kills hundreds of people instantly and wounds many others.

The sound of flapping wings high in the air as the fire burns brightly in the distance is unnerving. The beauty from above hides the dreadful truth of what lies on the ground behind. It's 700-miles from

Mexico City to Laredo, Texas. The owl is headed for the United States. This Christmas, Santa may be coming. But it is certain that *The Whistling Man* is coming to town. And, he is headed straight for the *Gateways to the Americas International Bridge* from Mexico—leading to Laredo, Texas—unabated and undetected.

Escape from Venezuela - 12:30 am

Chief Renier Rodriguez was wrapping up a late-night meeting with two foreign nations when his assistant burst into the room.

"Chief, I have some urgent news for you," the assistant announced determinedly and nervously.

"What is it? Can't you see I'm busy?" the Chief said in anger.

"You're gonna want to hear this, sir," he said.

"What is it?" Chief said reluctantly.

"Laurie Orsted escaped from the Caracas facility!"

"She what, Soldier?" the Chief asked in a very surprised voice.

"They just called and said she escaped, sir."

"Goddammit!" screamed the Chief, as he flung papers from his desk into the air.

"And where is she going, exactly?"

"I don't know, sir. They said she fled in a red Audi SQ7 SUV driven by a man."

"Jesus Christ! They are headed to Mexico!" the Chief screamed. "Do not let them leave Venezuela! Get me the hospital director on the phone, NOW!" Coincidentally, the two other men in the room with the Chief at that time were top Mexican military officials.

****

After exiting the hospital parking lot, Dizzy and Laurie knew they needed to get out of Venezuela quickly. No one appeared to have been immediately following them, which bought them only a little time. Laurie was now a very high-profile fugitive; a prestigious escapee. They knew it was only a matter of time before a country-wide manhunt would ensue.

"Where are we going?" Laurie asked.

"I have a friend at a private airstrip who owes me a favor," said Dizzy. "He is going to loan me his helicopter and we are going to fly to Mexico."

"Mexico?" Laurie asked. "I want to go home, home, to the United States."

"Yes, yes, little lady, I know. From Mexico, I have another friend who will be taking us to Texas. Then we will be safe."

"Oh, okay," Laurie said with relief. "So how do you know Daniela?"

"Well, I was in a local bar in Caracas one night and I saw this pretty lady there who looked familiar..."

One week earlier...

Dizzy enters his favorite local watering hole in downtown Caracas. It was a long day at work and he needed a drink. He walked over to the bar and took a seat.

"Dizzy!" the bartender said with admiration. Dizzy is like a celebrity in Caracas. He stands out like a sore thumb and is quite entertaining.

"I need a shot of whiskey, some beer

nuts, and a million dollars," said Dizzy.

"Well, I have whiskey and beer nuts. Can't help you with the million dollars."

"Two outta three ain't bad, I'll take 'em," Dizzy said. The bartender laughed and brought Dizzy beer nuts and his favorite drink, Whiskey on the rocks. Dizzy takes a sip and notices a very pretty woman sitting alone at a table nearby. Dizzy covertly observes her for a few moments and then decides to approach.

"Hey there, darlin. You look mighty familiar. Have we met?"

"I don't think so," she said, sounding a bit caught off guard.

"Now, I don't forget faces. Especially ones that are prettier than a speckled pup under a wagon with its tongue hanging out." The woman blushes. "Wait a darn second! You're that nurse over at the psychiatric facility, aren't you?" Dizzy said, surprised.

"Why, yes. How do you know that?" she asked.

"Cause I was over there bout a month ago. I'm the one who picked up that girl, Laurie, and was with her in the ER, and then at the psych hospital."

"Oh my!" she said, stunned. "Why were you with her?"

"Because her and her friends hired me to drop them off in Pavoso and pick them up. And when I picked her up, she was in bad shape. So, I took her to the hospital. I sat with her, and then a military guy came and took us both to the psych hospital. It was quite disturbing. I knew something was wrong with that situation."

"I know her well. I feel so bad for her. It's not right what they are doing to her." She says sympathetically. "She is not being treated well at all, and I fear they will kill her real soon. Like they do with many of the others in that ward."

"Kill her? Oh, dang it! They couldn't find their asses over there if they had both hands in their back pockets. Plus, I feel bad, cause I'm the one that got her in this mess. She's as lost as last year's Easter egg over there."

"If there was only something I could do," the nurse pondered.

"I got an idea," said Dizzy…

****

"So, we got to talking," said Dizzy, "and we devised this plan. And spending all that time together for the last couple of weeks, we grew close. And now we're an item."

"You are dating Daniela?" Laurie asked, shocked.

"I am. And she makes me as happy as a clam at high tide."

"Well, that's great," she said. "She is a good woman. But I'm afraid for her safety after this incident."

"Me too," said Dizzy, "but she is a smart cookie. I'm sure she will be fine for now. We will get her out of there before any of those dogs come sniffin. Right now, we need to skedaddle or we're both gonna be fish bate."

Race to Hanger 11

Laurie was amazed to find out about such a serendipitous meeting between Daniela and Dizzy; one that ultimately saved her life.

"How much farther until the airstrip?" Laurie asked as they merged onto the freeway, trying to avoid a down powerline.

"This is the *Autopista Francisco Fajardo Freeway*," said Dizzy.

"The what?" Laurie asked.

"It's the most important freeway in Caracas," Dizzy explained. "We are headed west. From here, we get off at the third exit and it's a straight shot, up north, to the private airstrip off *El Retiro*. And, as long as the creek don't rise, we will be out of here before you know it, darlin."

Only seconds later, several wailing sirens came whizzing from behind. Three cop cars and three army Humvees, light utility vehicles (LUVs), pull up aggressively behind their vehicle. Dizzy looks in his rearview mirror anxiously. Dizzy and Laurie sat in the middle lane of the three-lane highway.

A voice calls out from the cop car loud speaker, "Tú en el suv rojo, tire de su vehículo encima ahora."

"Oh, shit. What did he just say?" Laurie asks in fear.

"He said, 'You in the red SUV, pull your vehicle over now!' Hold on, darlin."

Dizzy floored it! He swerved from the middle lane into the left lane, narrowly missing the car in front of him in the middle lane and the car just a hair behind him in the fast lane. The cop cars and LUVs jockeyed for position, trying to keep up and pin Dizzy in. Laurie sinks into her seat and grabs a tight hold of the overhead handle. Dizzy remains as calm as a cucumber, as his vehicle builds in speed and energy. He swerves through traffic like a pro on the busy freeway. The blaring sirens from the cop cars are almost aiding him, as cars immediately in front of Dizzy hear them and move to the side.

WOOP, WOOP!

One of the cop cars screams as it pulls alongside Dizzy, on the passenger side. Both police in the car motion angrily for them to pull over. Dizzy looks at them and points at himself, acting as if he doesn't know what they are saying. "Me?" Dizzy says and gestures. He then swerves hard-right and rams the police car head-on into the back of a pedestrian-vehicle. The closest

LUV starts shooting at Dizzy and Laurie's vehicle from its mounted gun turret. However, instead of hitting its desired target, it hits two other pedestrian vehicles. The struck vehicles spin out, causing the LUV to turn sharply to its right, where it collides with one of the struck vehicles and flips several times, finally landing on its roof.

"Oh my God," Laurie screams. "We're gonna die!"

"Not today, little lady!" Dizzy says confidently. They pass the first exit going upwards of 140 mph. One of the cop cars manages to *ZOOM* past Dizzy in the right lane, as traffic clears a bit. The cop car maneuvers its way in front of Dizzy, trying to slow him down. Every time Dizzy tried to swerve and pass, the cop car countered.

They now had Dizzy boxed in.

"Oh, okay," Dizzy said in anger. "They are trying to sheepdog me. We invented this down south ya know?!" One of the LUVs rear-ended Dizzy, as the second cop car sped past. Dizzy was now wedged between a cop car and a LUV, slowing him to almost 70 mph. Dizzy maneuvered into the middle lane, trying to pass the cop car, to no avail. Dizzy sped hard to the left. The cop car responded, but overcompensated a bit to the left. Dizzy had only faked left. Once the cop car overcommitted left, Dizzy went hard right. He floored it! The cop compensated quickly, taking a hard-right angle, trying to end the chase right then and there. Dizzy swerved into the right lane and was just a bit ahead of the cop car. But he knew if he didn't clear the cop car completely, it would hit his rear driver's side and send him into a perilous spin. Dizzy angled even further right, heading onto the right shoulder of the freeway. He zoomed past the cop car, as the right side of his SUV lightly scraped the metal divider. The cop car was angled hard-right, expecting impact with the SUV. When the SUV avoided impact—darting past him—it caused the cop car to crash violently into the metal divider, sending it flipping over the divider and onto the grass.

Dizzy had just passed the second exit. He raced forward. The other cop car was way ahead by now. Two exits ahead more cops were waiting. They had also set spikes on the ground at the exit. Dizzy got his speed up again and raced toward the exit. The LUVs had a hard time keeping up with Dizzy's high-performance vehicle. Dizzy pulls out his cell phone and places a call.

"Horatio [*whore-racio*]?" said Dizzy.

"Yeah, where are you?"

"Listen close," Dizzy says. "I'm coming in hot! Leave the chopper running and get your tail outa there!"

"Roger that," said Horatio. "It's right outside Hanger 11. Godspeed Amigo!"

Dizzy is in the fast lane again. Traffic has picked up slightly. One of the LUVs had caught up to him and is now trailing close behind. The LUV prepared to fire its gun.

"The exit is coming up in 1/4th of a mile," Laurie mentioned. Dizzy paid her no mind. "Dizzy," she shouted, "the exit is coming up now, get over." Dizzy stayed stone-faced. The exit was coming up in seconds. The gun on the LUV was now locked on the target and ready to fire. Both the middle and slow lanes were now heavily congested. It appeared too late now for Dizzy to slow his speed and exit the freeway. Just then, Dizzy pulled the emergency brake, turned hard-right, and narrowly missed crashing into the car in the middle lane and the one in the slow lane. The side of his SUV slammed into the large yellow water barrels.

Boom!

It explodes. Water comes flying out. The right side of the SUV slams into a car on the exit, which actually helped, because it straightened the SUV out. Not so much for the other car though, which slammed into the wall on the right. The LUV that was following close behind was simply unable to make such a drastic turn. And was quite frankly shocked that Dizzy was able to. And, being that they thought Dizzy was headed to the international airport, which was one exit past the one Dizzy had gotten off at, they anticipated the wrong move.

Dizzy exited at *Avenida Baralt* going north. One LUV and one cop car were still, however, able to follow them and maintain a close distance.

"I don't know how we're going to make it out of this one," said Laurie.

"Well," Dizzy said. "We still got at least two more behind us. But have faith. I can drive anything with an engine better than just about anybody." Somehow Laurie did have faith in Dizzy's abilities. She had now witnessed them first-hand, not once but twice. As the vehicles closed in on Dizzy, he knew he had to make a move soon. Dizzy made a sharp right onto *Avenida Oeste 18.*

"I thought you said the airstrip was straight up *Avenida Baralt?"* said Laurie.

"I did," Dizzy responded.

"Then why did you turn off that street?"

"We need to lose these pigs or we're never gonna get off the ground," Dizzy said. Dizzy raced around traffic, hitting an unmanned newspaper stand. Papers flew everywhere, even on the cop car's front windshield. The cop and LUV held close behind. They radioed for backup once they realized that the destination was different from what they had anticipated. Five blocks up, Dizzy makes a left onto *Av Sur 5,* skidding and fishtailing. He turns hard into the fishtail and evens out. The sirens are still wailing and close behind.

One of the head Soldiers communicates the progress with Chief

Rodriguez.

"We thought that they were heading to the international airport, but they got off one exit before," the Soldiers relays.

"I want them dead or alive; do you hear me?" the Chief commands.

Dizzy gets his speed up again. Up ahead, one truck is backing out of a driveway slowly. Only a block ahead, another truck on the right is backing out slowly as well. Both are halfway onto Av Sur 5 on opposite sides.

"Woh, woh, woh!" Laurie screams as she sees the truck backing out. Dizzy turns the wheel slightly to the right (staying almost in the middle of the road), barely missing the back of the first truck. But, in doing so, he was able to make the correction to the left necessary to avoid the second truck.

Boom!

The final LUV slammed into the middle of the second truck, causing a major explosion. Flames shot out in every direction. The cop car had slowed significantly but managed to continue to give chase. Dizzy makes another hard-left, this time onto *Av Este 8*.

Dizzy sped down the street. He only now needed to get back to *Avenida Baralt* and continue straight for a few miles to reach the airstrip. However, a train emerged from underground, moving at a very high speed. It was now running parallel to them. The cop car closed in, and more cops joined from behind.

"What are we going to do?" Laurie asked.

"There is a road crossing just ahead," said Dizzy. "We need to beat this train to it."

"No way!" Laurie shouted. "That's suicide. This train is going way too fast." Dizzy was having trouble trying to get ahead of the express train. He floored it. The smell of burnt rubber can be smelt by onlookers. He gets ahead of the train slightly and begins to slowly increase his lead. However, the curved, crossing road was coming up fast. Dizzy got the SUV up to 150 mph. The vehicle was shaking.

"We're not gonna make it," Laurie screamed. "We are not gonna make it!"

Dizzy slowed a bit and veered right

onto *Retorno Avenida 8*. Even the train's conductor braced for impact. Laurie looked at the front of the train, which was about to hit her head-on, on the passenger side.

'Wait,' she shouted with her inner voice. The train and everything but the SUV seemed to have been in suspended animation for a split second, as the SUV soared onto the other side of the train. The cop had stopped, realizing that he was not going to make it. That split second turned back to real-time quickly.

"Woo hoo!" Dizzy shouted. "Did you see that?"

"Yeah, you almost got us killed!" Laurie said.

"It was almost like time slowed down, but we kept moving in real-time," Dizzy said. He was confused, although, his adrenaline was pumping and his mind had not caught up yet. They made a sharp left onto *Av Oeste 6*, and then a sharp right back onto *Avenida Baralt.* They had bought themselves a little time.

A few miles north, they made a right onto *Calle 3 El Retiro*. Within a minute after that, they had reached the entrance to the private airstrip. They raced to hanger 11. There, the helicopter was already running and ready to fly. They ran to the chopper and got strapped in. Cop cars and military vehicles raced onto the scene trying to thwart their escape. However, the helicopter was in flight in only seconds. Chief Rodriguez was among those at the airstrip. He exited his vehicle in time to see the chopper abruptly lift off.

"Damnit!" he shouted, as he threw his beret to the ground. One Soldier close by picked it up for him. "Get me Obrador [President of Mexico] on the phone, now!" the Chief screamed. "And get some helicopters in the sky and hunt them down! I want those bastard's dead!"

Chapter 7

Chopper Inflight

"Where are we headed?" Laurie asks.

"We are headed over yonder to Monterrey, Mexico. We are gonna meet my buddy, Jack, and he is going to hide the chopper and get it back to Horatio [*whore-racio*]. Jack will get us safely into Texas. He's a coyote."

"A what?" Laurie asks.

"A person that smuggles people from Mexico into the U.S," Dizzy responds.

"And how long of a ride is it to Monterrey?"

"Well, this here is a *Eurocopter X3*, the fastest helicopter in the world," Dizzy boasted. "Its top speed is 295MPH, which is what I intend on doing the whole way there, pretty much. We have about twenty-four-hundred miles to go. So, I reckon it will take us a little more than eight hours to arrive."

"And how will I get into the U.S.?" Laurie asks. "Everything I had brought with me was left in the cabin in Pavoso, including my passport."

"Yes, I know," said Dizzy. "The government used it to prove your death. They showed it on TV."

"Oh, how nice," Laurie said sarcastically. "And what if that military guy comes after us?"

"I'm gonna fly us under the detection of radar, so they won't be hot on our tale."

"Listen, Dizzy," Laurie said. "I really want to thank you for what you are doing."

"Say no more, little lady. I was thinking of retiring anyway and heading back to the states. You actually helped me." Laurie chuckles.

"What are we going to do about

Daniela?" asked Laurie.

"She's fixin to meet us in Texas in a day or two."

"Do you know this Jack guy very well?" Laurie asked.

"We were in the army together. We are both from the south and buddied-up in the military and have stayed in touch ever since. That kinda bond don't fade. And he is as funny and as crazy as all get-out. He moved down here at the same time I did. He is partnered up with some of the U.S. Ice Agents. He smuggles in Mexicans illegally. He makes a killing too."

"Wow," said Laurie, "and he literally gets away with doing that to make a living?"

"Look at it this way," said Dizzy. "Most of these human traffickers are thieves and, you know, and the other half, well, give them two nickels for a dime and they'll think they rich, you know; they're not that bright. A lot of their loads get busted, meaning all those who paid a lot of money are not only sent back to Mexico, they're sent back after losing their life savings as well. Old Jack is a safe play. And the border patrol can regulate what gets in.

Plus, Jack helps them snuff out the competition by giving them information on other smugglers."

"And the U.S. Government is okay with this?" Laurie asks.

"Look here, you really think the U.S. Government doesn't want illegals? Hell, the whole U.S. economy would collapse without em. Ain't no U.S. citizen gonna wash dishes for a living for two dollars an hour. You can say they overlook a few things here and there."

"I guess that makes sense," said Laurie. "Man, I've learned more about the world in the last few months than in my whole life. It's all corruption, through and through, that runs everything. Wrong and right are just illusions."

"You bet your sweet petunias," said Dizzy. "Anyone who thinks otherwise is about as useless as a screen door on a submarine. It will be morning when we get to Monterrey. You look worn slap out, darlin. Why don't you get some sleep? You're gonna need your rest." Laurie lays back on the seat, eyes open, pondering the new world she had just discovered.

****

Monterrey Jack

{Daytime-10am} The dark-haired American man in the blue-wool poncho walks through a busy street market in Monterrey, Mexico. The street market has everything from fresh fruit stands, to cheap clothing, to antojitos (literally "little cravings") and much more, all prepared by street vendors. The savory aromas in the air tantalize the receptors in the nose. The aroma from the amalgamation of the assortment of foods—tacos, tamales, quesadillas, tostadas, empanadas, fajitas, tortas, pambazo, nachos, chilaquiles, gorditas, empalmes, chalupas, and much more—fill the air in the streets.

The man in the blue-wool poncho appears to be in a hurry. He slithers through the crowd, nearly bumping shoulders with slow-walking pedestrians in his path. He stops at a fruit stand. Everywhere you look there are different fruits. Stacks of bananas and pineapples tower above all else, sitting high on the shelves above.

"So, where are they?" he asks the curator of the stand in a southern United States accent.

"You told me yesterday that you weren't leaving for another twenty minutes from now?" the curator said in angst.

"I'm on a strict schedule, here, okay?" the American announced firmly. "When I tell you a time, that is the time. I gotta go!"

"But Jack," the man said stammering. "After all I've done for you?"

"I'm just busting your balls, Poncho Via," Jack teased, as he cracked a devilish smile. The curator lets out a sigh of relief. "Give me a little more this time, okay," Jack says, referring to the bag of fruits he gets before every trip. "I have a heavy load today." The truck ride from Monterrey to Laredo is about two-and-and-half hours, plus the long line at the *Gateways to the Americas International Bridge*. Along with a first-class ticket to Texas—which consists of sitting in the back of a truck, with a bunch of others, with no light or view of the outside terrain (which is still considered first-class, relatively speaking)—Jack also provides his passengers with some fresh fruits and bottled water for the trip. The curator places more fruits in the bag and hands Jack the sack.

"Make sure your flunkies are at the truck in twenty minutes," Jack warned.

"Yes sir, Mr. Jack, sir."

Jack hurries back through the crowd, on his way back to the truck. He, again, slithers his way through the crowd.

Nudge!

He unintendedly slams shoulders with a Mexican man, who appeared ready for the impact. Jack's shoulder swings back. "Sorry about—" but he stops abruptly when he sees who bumped into him. The man, wearing a black Jaguar warrior pullover hoodie with an Aztec design in gold down the left sleeve and onto the left chest area, stares at him with contempt.

"You should wash whay ju going, Ese," the man says, using very poor English. "Wan day ju might run intau de rung porson."

"What's wrong, Paco?" asked Jack. "Your boss lose his leash?" The two muscular men behind Paco take an aggressive step forward. Paco puts his right hand up, signaling for them to halt, and they do.

"Ju know, pendejo," Paco said in disgust, "chore day es kalming. And dime gonna be da won who bulls de trigga when dat dae comz."

"Paco, I know you think the sun comes up just to hear you crow," said Jack. "But—"

"Why don't chew faking speaka Engleesh, Mang."

"Me?" Jack says, as he giggles. "Look, I have an arrangement with your boss. So, unless something has changed, you and your hounds need to move out of my way?"

Paco puts his right hand out sideways and motions it backward, signaling for his men to step aside.

"Thank you," said Jack. "Say hello to your wife for me," Jack says sarcastically, as he scurries by the men. Again, the two muscular men want to attack Jack. Again, Paco halts them.

"Paciencia; sus dias estan contados." ("Patience; his days are numbered.")

Coyote Ugly (*9:30 am*)

The Eurocopter X3 lands at its designated spot in Monterrey.

"Laurie, Laurie!" Dizzy calls out. Laurie opens her eyes from a deep sleep and sits up brusquely. "We're here. Let's get a move on before any trouble finds us." They exit the helicopter and run around back.

"Where are we going?" Laurie asked.

"Over there," Dizzy said, pointing to a beat-up light blue and white pickup truck. "That's our ride." They ran over to the vehicle. Dizzy opens the driver's side door.

"But you don't have the keys," Laurie mentions. "Are you going to hotwire it?" Dizzy looks under the driver's side floor mat. He pulls out a shiny jingling object.

"Will these do?" he says, holding up two silver keys on a silver keychain. Laurie shrugs her shoulders and enters via the passenger door.

Laurie and Dizzy arrived a bit early. They hustle over to the meeting spot. Several future Central American migrants gathered around a large *Praga V3S* military vehicle, which has a large back section to carry several passengers and what looks like a curtain draped over the back to conceal the passengers.

Dizzy recognizes Jack right away.

"Does anyone here know where I can find an ugly gringo coyote?" Dizzy announces. Several people stare at Dizzy with contempt for the comment, not being sure what to make of it. Jack turned; his eyes widened from the surprise of who he was looking at. A smile immediately dawned on his face. They rushed each other, ending in a joyous embrace. The tension of the angry onlookers immediately subsided, and they went back to doing whatever it was they were doing prior.

"You old dog, you!" Jack shouted.

"You're about as pretty right now as a mess of fried catfish," said Dizzy. The reacquaintance was grand. Everyone near saw, including some dubious witnesses nearby. Paco and his cronies were in the vicinity and saw the reunion. The look on Paco's face was one of satisfaction, believing he was witnessing some precious cargo.

"This is Laurie," said Dizzy.

"Oh, I know who this is," said Jack. "She is well known around the world, especially these parts. Here, take these." Jack handed them two ponchos he had prepared for them. Laurie's had a hood on it. They put them on promptly.

"It's been so long, my friend," said Dizzy. "I'm as happy to see you as a dead pig in the sunshine."

"Me too," Jack said. "I'm as thrilled as tight pants on a hooker, my friend." They both smiled and looked into each other's eyes for a moment. "Walk with me."

"I'll be right back," Dizzy says to Laurie. Dizzy and Jack walk away to talk in private.

"I heard what happened," said Jack. "Are you gonna be okay?"

"Sure," said Dizzy. "As long as I get to Texas, I'll be fine."

"This situation just makes my ass itch," said Jack. "What they did to that girl is criminal."

"Yeah," said Dizzy, "they sure licked the red off her candy."

"Well, I'm gonna get ya'll outa here in about twenty minutes, tops," Jack promised. "That border is about to open up for you two like a two-dollar hooker you just gave ten dollars." Dizzy laughs. "Can I get you anything while you wait?"

"I'm so hungry, my belly thinks my throat's been cut," said Dizzy. "We're gonna go over to the street fair and grab a bite right quick."

"Okay," Jack said. "just mind your P's and Q's, and get back here right away." Dizzy hurried over to Laurie. "Are you hungry," he asked.

"I'm starving," Laurie retorts. "I can go for some sushi."

"Sushi?" Dizzy says with a distressed look on his face. "Down south, sushi is still bait. Plus, sushi in Mexico is very different than in Japan or the U.S. It's got a Mexican feel to it."

"What does that mean?" Laurie asked.

"It's spicy, crunchy, cream cheese-slathered, and at times, beefy." Dizzy shrugs his shoulders. "I need real food!"

"Okay, fine," said Laurie. "But I need

a burner phone before we do anything. I need to call James as soon as possible."

"Okay, let's hurry," said Dizzy.

At the same time the two scurried off, Chief Renier Rodriguez and twenty armed men—most Venezuelan Soldiers, and a few Mexican police officers—arrived in Monterrey. The Chief was well-known in Mexico. His presence, even well out of his jurisdiction, caused fear. The Chief and his Soldiers marched through the fare. People moved out of the way quickly when they saw him coming.

"Have you seen this woman?" the Chief asked one vendor, showing her a picture of Laurie.

"No, no, boss."

"Don't lie to me," the Chief cautioned. "There will be dire consequences."

"I have not, I swear," she responded in fear. The Chief and his Soldiers marched through, asking several other market attendants. Suddenly, Paco and his men approached the Chief.

"Chief Rodriguez," Paco said in Spanish, in which he speaks fluently. "I have seen the girl and her American friend. They are on the dirt road over there in an army truck with a coyote named Jack, also an American."

"Lead the way," said the Chief.

Jack had just arrived back at the truck, after retrieving the fruits.

"Can I help you?" Jack asked the Chief.

"I'm here on special orders of the President," the Chief said. "I've been told that you are harboring an important fugitive of Venezuela." Jack looked at Paco, who had a devilish grin.

"From who?" asked Jack. "This cartel member who is trying to put me out of business?" Jack said, pointing to Paco.

"Cartel?" said Paco. "I'm not cartel. I'm just a concerned citizen."

"I simply need to check your vehicle," said the Chief. "If they are not here, we will be on our way."

"Sure, go ahead," Jack stated. Paco's eyes widened in anticipation. But he also realized the confidence in Jack.

"I saw them here Chief," Paco pleaded. "He is pulling a fast one; I know it."

Dizzy and Laurie were eating tacos and walking back to the truck after buying the phone when Dizzy saw the commotion.

"Oh, shit," said Dizzy. He grabbed Laurie and they ducked behind a food truck.

"They're not here," a Soldier reported to the Chief.

"Are you rousing me, boy?" the Chief asked Paco.

"No, no," Paco pleaded. "I saw them here only a few moments ago."

"Maybe it is him who is harboring the fugitive, sir," Jack suggests.

"Where is your truck?" the Chief asked.

"I don't have a truck," Paco insisted.

"It's over there," Jack said, pointing to a food truck that was loading passengers.

"Is that your truck?" the Chief asked, now suspicious from Paco's lies.

"Yes," Paco said reluctantly. "But it is just to transport food within Mexico. Not headed for the states."

"Well then, you wouldn't mind me searching it then, would you?" the Chief asked. Jack looked at Paco and snuck in a vengeful smile.

"No, of course not," said Paco, as his face sunk in despair. "But I assure you, it is he who harbors the fugitives."

"Yeah, okay," the Chief said. "Let's take a look at that vehicle of yours, shall we?" They marched swiftly over to Paco's vehicle.

"Let's get this truck out of here," Jack told the two U.S. Border Patrol officers in charge of driving the vehicle. "Remember," Jack told them, "Terminal 3 only at the bridge." The officers both nodded their heads up and down and headed for the truck. Jack looked over and saw Dizzy peaking from behind the stand out of the corner of his eye. Jack gave him a signal using his hand—a shared communication they had learned from their U.S. Army days—to meet further up the road. Dizzy got it and nodded back in acceptance. However, as the truck was pulling away, Laurie grabbed Dizzy's arm and said, "Come with me." She put her head down and walked slowly toward the truck.

"What are you doing?" Dizzy asked. "Do you have a death wish?" Dizzy jerked, releasing his arm from her grip.

"Just keep walking," Laurie said, grabbing hold of his arm again. However, it did not sound like Laurie's voice; not even close. It shook and confused Dizzy, in fact. He followed. Dizzy put his head down but looked around to see if anyone was keen on their presents. He saw something that confused him even further. He was perplexed to see the people around them moving unusually slowly, like slow-motion, even; while he and Laurie seemed to be walking at normal speed. When they arrived at the truck, the Soldier sitting at the back looked at them funny.

"How the hell did you guys get over here so fast; did you fly?" He helped them onto the truck, which was moving very slowly at the time. Once the two were on board, the Soldier at the back banged twice on the metal wall inside the truck and the truck sped off immediately. Paco and his cronies were being put into handcuffs, much to their objections, as the truck raced up the road toward the sun.

Chapter 8

Fire in the Sky

It's a sunny day in Laredo, Texas. The high for the day was forecasted to be 65°F, the low 43°F. It was about 60°F at 1:00 pm. At a nearby local gas station, Travis was behind the register in the room to the left, and Rufus, the mechanic was all greased up in his overalls giving a car an oil change in the garage in the center room of the station. The beginning of the song, *I'm Going Down*, by *Bruce Springsteen* had just started playing loudly on the transistor radio in the garage. The car was lifted off the ground about seven feet high so that Rufus could get underneath it. Across the street, a horned owl sat on a power line way above the street. There are seventeen documented owl species in Texas. And although the great horned owl is primarily nocturnal, no one in that vicinity at that time would have been paying much mind to the species, much less an owl in general. A dozen or so crows are circling the gas station and cawing loudly.

Rufus was underneath the car unscrewing the cap to release the oil into the pan below when a whizzing sounded behind him. He turned and saw the owl fly, very fast, into the shop area to his left, the far-right room of the station. He put the rag he was holding over his left shoulder, with his right hand, and walked cautiously over to the shop doorway. He peeks in but sees no owl. He slowly walks into the shop and sees that the small walk-in shed is open. Rufus looks befuddled, as it's never open. He has OCD and always checks that sort of thing several times. Such a thing can trigger him into an anxiety-filled event. He walks into the shed and looks around. While he is there, he decides to grab one of the wrenches he will need for later. But the door suddenly closes while he is inside.

Being claustrophobic, Rufus quickly tries to open the French-style doors. But he was met with great resistance. He even began shoulder-blocking the doors with a two-step running start, using his right shoulder to provide greater impact. Yet, it wouldn't budge. The fact that there was no lock on the door, whatsoever, baffled the mechanic.

"Who in the fuck is out there?" He screamed. "Are you fucking with me, Travis?" he shouted. But there was no answer. Rufus was much tougher than Travis, and certainly held the dominant role in their relationship. This was out of character of Travis, but Rufus felt this as a power grab. "Okay, you wanna play boy, playboy? Get ready, cause I'm coming with some linebacker shit right now!" He paused for a moment and caught his breath. "One," he announced, "two," he said, "Three!" he yelled. Rufus thrusts forward with all his might. This time, however, there was no resistance. Rufus blasts through the doors. He anticipated strong resistance, but receiving none. This caused him to stumble as he flew through the doors and fall to the ground, twisting around in midair and landing on his back; his feet closest to the shed. Aside from the whole ordeal being disconcerting, Rufus needed a second to get his bearings. Making matters slightly worse, he had hit his head on the ground, which blurred his vision slightly.

"Travis, is that you?" Rufus called out, seeing a blurred figure straddling his head area and looking down at him. "You think this shit was funny, boy?" Rufus shakes his head to try and see a bit better. "Oh, now you're a tough guy, is that it?" Rufus said in anger. The figure raised both arms, holding a steel crowbar with both hands, and brings it down with extreme force onto Rufus's head. The crunching of bones is the pervasive sound as Rufus's skull is crushed with one single, fatal blow.

The phone rings up front.

"Hello, how can I help you?" Asks Travis. "Oh, hi Mrs. Jennings. [pause] I'm not sure. Let me go ask Rufus." Travis puts Mrs. Jennings on hold and walks toward the garage area. The song, *Sympathy for the Devil*, by *The Rolling Stones,* had just begun ("*Please allow me to introduce myself...*"). Travis lights a cigarette as he walks into the garage area. "Rufus," he called out. "Rufus." He had to scream because the radio was loud. He took a few steps into the garage. He took a puff of his cigarette as his eyes were looking straight ahead. He caught a peripheral image below, however. His eyes panned down. There he saw Rufus in the fetal position, lying underneath the raised car, wearing only white (Fruit of the Loom) underwear. Travis dropped his cigarette, unconsciously. He was filled with shock and horror. The cigarette hits the ground and rolls toward the large garage doors. Travis instinctively runs over to Rufus's body to see if he was still breathing. He kneels beside the body on one knee. "Rufus," he shouts, as he shakes his left shoulder. "Rufus," again he shouts, as he grabs his left shoulder and pulls on him. Rufus's body rolls toward Travis, and lands on his back.

Immediately, he saw that Rufus's

forehead was completely caved in, and blood was pouring out. He also saw Rufus's stomach was gutted. Scanning the body further, he saw that a bone had been ripped from his left leg. He was shocked and devastated. So much so, that he didn't even look around or protect himself from an ambush from a potential attacker. Travis's mind is racing. He is completely unaware of his surroundings. However, while he was focused on grief and confusion, he didn't realize that he wasn't alone. He heard a few soft footsteps and turned around swiftly. There, was the creature, standing right by the car-release-lever.

"What the...who the fuck are you?" Travis asks aggressively, with tears in his eyes. The figure stood wearing Rufus's greasy, grey overalls and also his—coincidentally—navy blue zip-up hoodie with the hood over his head. The figure just stood there, silent, no response. "What the hell, man?" Travis screamed. "Did you do this?" Again, the creature stands motionless. "Okay," Travis said frustratingly, "I'm calling the police." Travis stood up. The creature put his hand on the lever. Travis froze. He looked up.

"Wait, man!" he shouted, putting his right hand up, palm facing the figure. Both of them paused for a second. Then, the creature jerked the lever aggressively. That released the car from what was holding it up. Travis screamed and looked up again while putting his hands up over his head this time. Nonetheless, the quickly falling vehicle came crashing down on him, rapidly flattening Travis like a pancake. It was like one second he was there and the next he was violently and awkwardly taken down by the weight and velocity of the vehicle. His bones broke; his body folded in directions it was not made to.

Bam!

The crashing sound was intense and loud. The car windows smashed. The bottom of the wheels looked as if they were deflating as they slammed onto the concrete. However, they bounced back swiftly and bounced again. After a few bounces, it sat motionlessly.

The crash had knocked over a five-hundred-gallon fuel tank full of gas. Because the locking ball valve was not turned off, and the manual cap was not screwed on, the gas began spewing out, headed for the large garage doors at the front of the establishment. The creature stood there for a second as if admiring his own work. Blood began flowing from underneath the car in all directions.

By now, the lit cigarette had rolled to its present resting place. It was now resting against a broom that was leaning against the garage door. The broom had a few paper gas station receipts underneath it. The receipts slowly caught fire. Within a few minutes, the fire began raging up the wooden broom handle. The spilled gasoline rolled quickly toward the fire. Some of the spill had even rolled underneath the garage door, headed quickly for the gas pumps.

The creature walked back into the main area. "Hello? Hello? Is anyone there?" he heard the voice of Mrs. Jennings shout. The monster walked out the front door with the hood placed firmly over his head to conceal his face. As he walked past the gas pumps and into the street, two cars pulled in to get gas. The heavy-set-man, in the first car, got out of his vehicle. He looked at the creature in confusion, as the creature stepped up onto the curb across the street and continued walking away from the gas station.

"Hey Rufus," the heavy-set-man shouted. "Where are you headed?" But the creature just kept walking. "Say hello to Trixie for me," he shouted. The man walked in to pay for his gas. He opened the door. "What's that smell?" he said aloud. "Travis, are you here? I'm in a hurry."

The woman in the car behind the heavy-set man's car looked out her left passenger window and saw flames raging in the garage area. Her mouth opened wide from shock and panic. She started beeping repeatedly at first. Then, she backed up furiously, and quickly put the car in drive. She saw a wide trail of gas rapidly approaching her car and a trail of fire approaching right behind it coming from the garage area. She stepped on the gas with all her might. Her wheels spun out, causing her tires to scream. The heavy-set man inside walked back outside and saw the fire. "Oh shit!" he said, as he began to run in the opposite direction.

BOOM!

The heavy-set man was eviscerated by the flames immediately. The woman's car had started moving forward just as the explosion hit, causing her car to explode as it zoomed forward. Engulfed in flames and traveling at a high velocity, the car crashed through the house next to the gas station, causing the house to go ablaze. Several explosions resulting in large clouds of smoke and fire filled the air for miles. The creature did not even turn to look. He just continued walking casually as the fire in the sky raged on.

Chapter 9

A Call to Arms (1:00 pm)

The five-ton LMTV, with its camo cargo bed cover and frame, raced toward the *Gateway to the Americas International Bridge* that leads to Laredo, Texas. Twenty-five people had been stuffed into the back of the truck, including Laurie and Dizzy. The truck was quiet for most of the ride. The majority of passengers used the time to nap. Their long trip to get to the truck then to this point had proven exhausting and laborious.

Dizzy had dozed off as well. Laurie pulls out the burner phone she recently purchased and dials. One ring, two rings, three rings...her heart raced faster with every ring. Every pause in between rings felt like hours.

On the fifth ring, a man answered, "Hello?"

"James?" Laurie asked in a desperate voice.

"Who's this?" the man asked.

"It's Laurie," she said, as she burst into tears.

"Laurie?" he asked, confused and shocked.

"It's me, James!" she said firmly in a crying, muffled voice.

"Laurie? Is that you?" he asked, excited and worried.

"James, I've missed you so much," she said.

"Oh my God, I thought you were dead," he says with relief. "Where are you?" he asked decisively.

"I have so much to tell you, but first I need your help. I don't have much time."

"Okay, okay, anything," he said.

"I escaped from a psychiatric facility in Venezuela, and I'm being chased by police. I'm currently in Mexico on a truck headed for Laredo Texas. I need a ride and a place to stay, and please tell no one!"

"Of course," he said. "You can count on me. Anything you need, I'm here for you." James had serendipitously moved to

Washington County, Texas only a couple of years before. So, he was just under five hours from Laredo, Texas.

"I'm on my way!" he said. "Call me soon and let me know where to meet you."

"Okay," she said. "And James?"

"Yes?" he asked.

"Thank you, and I miss you!"

"Me too," he said. "I'm on my way! Just get there safely and call me with your location!" Laurie hangs up the phone and notices that one of the only other stowaways on the truck is still awake. He is sitting across from her and one seat to her left, and he is starring at her.

"Can I help you with something?" Laurie asks sarcastically.

"You are Laurie," he says with a thick Spanish accent, "the girl on the news; the one who beat El Silbón."

"No!" Laurie said adamantly. "You must have me confused with someone else."

"Oh, no," he responded, "no confusion. You're her. It's okay, I'm a big fan. I'm glad to see you're alive."

"That makes two of us," said Laurie.

"You know, they saying you have magic powers," he remarks.

"Who are 'they?'" she asks.

"Everyone! No one confronts the monster and lives to tell about it."

"I'm just lucky, I guess," she says. Laurie is not very engaged. She is not on this trip to make friends. Moreover, being the most wanted fugitive in Venezuela at the moment, she wants no part of this conversation. However, the man presses on.

"I'm Cortés," the man says, pointing to himself. "I practice what you in America call voodoo. I can sense in you a great presence."

"You have a great imagination," Laurie utters.

"No, no," he says, as he puts his hand on Laurie's leg, "it will consume you if you don't get a hold of it soon." Laurie looks down at his hand. It makes her very uncomfortable. She gets a sudden rush of indignation. She looks up at him, with his hand still on her thigh. Her eyes suddenly start glowing, emanating a bright red light. Cortés moves his hand away quickly,

"Ouch," he says, as he shakes his hand, trying to relieve the pain. Laurie's eyes quickly turn back to normal.

"I'm, I'm sorry, I'm sorry," she says, stammering from embarrassment and confusion.

"That's quite alright. Don't worry about it." Dizzy had awoken with the sudden jolt from Cortés, who was sitting next to Dizzy, on his right.

"What the taco Tuesday is going on here?" Dizzy asked in anger.

"It's nothing," said Laurie. "I was just speaking to Cortés here."

"Cortés, huh?" said Dizzy.

"Yes, Hernán Cortés," he answered, "but my amigos just call me Cortés."

"You mean like the old conquistador who defeated the Aztecs?" Dizzy asked.

"Si Señor. I'm a big fan of Laurie, much like everyone here. None of us like the establishment or Chief Rodriguez." The Soldier in the passenger seat pulls back the curtain. "We are ten minutes from the bridge," the Soldier relays. "We will likely be on line for an hour, so please be patient."

Ten minutes later, the truck pulls up

to the *Gateway to the Americas International Bridge*. The bridge connects Mexico to Laredo, Texas over the *Rio Grande* river. The line for Terminal 3 (the third terminal from the left) is, as the Soldier said, about an hour wait. Jack had ordered them to go to Terminal 3 only because that is the terminal that Jack had bribed the Soldier in the booth. In fact, Jack had a working relationship with him and a couple of other booth workers. He spread it around, making sure that one was not neglected over another. There was plenty of money to go around. Jack had several runs each day.

The group sat and waited patiently on a long line of cars and trucks. It wasn't that cold, but sitting in the truck without insulation for hours was getting to the stowaways. As they crept forward very slowly, an approaching helicopter could be heard, getting louder and louder.

Chuff chuff chuff chuff...

One of the stowaways pulled back the cover at the back of the truck.

"Oh mierda, es el jefe!" he shouted.

"What is it?" Laurie asked anxiously.

"Oh, Dingleberry pie, he just said, it's the Chief!" said Dizzy.

"We need to get you out of here now," said Cortés.

"He's fixin to carve us up like a turkey on Thanksgiving," said Dizzy.

No sooner did the chopper land than Chief Rodriguez and ten of his Soldiers had boots on the ground. They headed straight for the long lines of cars and trucks. All eyes were on the military personnel. Everyone knew something big was occurring.

"Spread out and find that truck!" the Chief ordered. Five followed the Chief to the left, five went off to the right. There are eight terminal booths. Once a person is lucky enough to get past one of these booths, they must merge onto the four lanes bridge leading into Texas.

The Chief and his five Soldiers spread out between the first four-terminal lanes. The other five did the same for four through eight. They started at the back of each lane and covertly worked their way forward, carefully observing each vehicle along the way. They tried to remain as stealth as possible, ducking low as they jogged up each lane, armed with M4 Carbine assault rifles.

One of the Chief's crew spotted Jack's truck. The Chief radioed to the rest of the group.

"All Soldiers to Terminal 3. We have located the target."

They crept up on the truck, using military hand signals to coordinate their movements. The Chief signaled for five of his Soldiers to position themselves in the front and five to do the same in the back. The Chief walked up to the passenger side door and aimed his rifle at the seated Soldier.

"I'm here on orders of the Mexican president," he said firmly." We are seeking a high-level fugitive named Laurie Orsted. Is she a passenger on this vehicle?"

"There is no person by that name on our vehicle, Chief," said the Soldier.

"Then you wouldn't mind if we take a look?" he asked.

"Go right ahead," the Soldier said. The Chief walked to the back of the vehicle. Two of the Soldiers hopped up and roughly searched the passengers.

Meanwhile, Laurie and Dizzy were being led toward the Rio Grande by Cortés. They had a nice head start and ducked low as they weaved through cars on their way to the right bank that led to the river. After searching the vehicle, and realizing that Laurie was not on board, the Chief quickly scanned the area. "There they are!" he screamed, seeing them crouching and heading down to the river bank. Their bodies began disappearing from waist to head as they traveled downward. "Fire!" the Chief screamed. His Soldiers began shooting, missing Dizzy by inches, as he was the last to head down.

People began screaming, as they ducked down in their vehicles, hiding for their lives.

"After them!" the Chief screamed.

"This way!" shouted Cortés. "Stay close to the bridge." The Rio Grande is about three feet deep at its highest point around the bridge. There were people all around barbequing and throwing balls around, and even some people in the water. Several U.S. Border Patrol Officers guarded the area from within the crowd, with their dogs in hand, looking for those that might try to use the opportunity to cross over into the United States. Cortés, followed by Laurie and Dizzy, made their way hastily across the Rio Grande, on the right side of the bridge. Once across, they tried to blend in with the crowd. They fast-walked through, trying not to be spotted by border police.

The Chief's Soldiers, however, were not so lucky. As soon as the first two Venezuelan Soldiers took a step out of the water and onto U.S. soil, six U.S. Border Patrol Officers ran toward the water and drew their guns. Screams can be heard, as people fled in every direction. Some stood nearby to witness the event.

"Freeze!" one of the patrol officers shouted. The Venezuelan Soldiers drew their guns in response. Dogs began barking and growling ferociously, with their teeth showing. The Chief and more Venezuelan Soldiers came running up seconds later. "State your business here?" another border patrol officer commanded.

"We are here on the orders of the Mexican President," the Chief announced.

"We are chasing a prison escapee and two men who aided her."

"Do you have clearance to come into the United States?" Another border patrol officer asked.

"That fugitive must be stopped at all costs!" the Chief commanded.

"Hey poncho," said the fourth border patrol officer, "You wanna start a war right now, do ya? Cause right now we got an international incident on our hands here. Now if you don't put those God-damned guns down, and I mean now, you will be facing a situation that you will not come back from!"

"Guns down, Soldiers!" the Chief ordered.

"Now, you best get yourselves back to Mexico," the same border patrol officer said. "We will find them and have them extradited if necessary." The Chief knew there was nothing further he could do. Laurie was gone. International rules would never allow for such an extradition unless she was formally charged with the Pavoso murders. But the fact that the Venezuelan government had claimed that she was dead, made their case null and void, unless they could come up with a very good bullshit story, and fast. The Chief and his Soldiers walked back into Mexico, defeated. With all the commotion going on, Cortés, Laurie, and Dizzy had managed to slither through the crowd unnoticed, somewhat.

They scurried up to route 170.

"Where do we go now?" Laurie asked.

"There's a *Holiday Inn* not far from the golf resort," said Dizzy. "We need to hitch a ride, cause we're talkin bout thirty miles from here, and we need to get off the streets, cause they'll be looking for us." Just then, a white border patrol pickup truck spotted them and pulled alongside and rolled down his passenger window.

"Can I have a word with yawl for a minute?" the officer asked kindly.

"Howdy, officer," Dizzy responded. The officer exited the vehicle and walked around to the front. He was wearing an all-brown police uniform with a straw cowboy hat on and dark sunglasses.

"You guys coming down from the party?" the officer asked, referring to the party by the bridge that the group had used to luckily stay concealed long enough to get to this point. "Because I see that you are all pretty wet from the waist down." A large snake slithered across the street, about five yards from them.

"We were most certainly at that shindig, officer (Dizzy looks at his nametag) McDonald," he replies.

"Did you go onto the Mexican side at all?"

"We did, just for a few moments, sir," said Laurie. This was a mistake by her, and the other two knew it.

"Hmm, okay," Officer McDonald says, as a navy blue and white pickup truck pulls over on the opposite side of the road. The truck reads, "Sheriff" on the driver's side and passenger's side doors. Four snakes slither across the street in the same direction as the other one did, toward the Sheriff's truck.

"Okay, well, you guys are in violation of 19-USC fourteen-fifty-nine, which is a Class A Misdemeanor." The sheriff exits his vehicle and starts walking over to them, making sure to avoid the snakes.

"What's going on over here?" the sheriff asks.

"We got a violation of 19-USC fourteen-fifty-nine," says Officer McDonald.

"You seeing all these snakes?" the sheriff asks, a bit unnerved. "Is it like snake mating season or something?"

"Actually, I heard there was an infestation in the area," said Laurie. "And they are very aggressive if you are near their home."

"Are you like a snake charmer or something?" the sheriff asked.

"Something like that," Laurie responded flippantly. Just then, about ten snakes came slithering from the side of the road and four of them wrapped around each leg of the two officers. The other snakes rose up and hissed at the officers.

"What the...," the border officer said in shock. Dizzy and Cortés froze in awe. Laurie remained stone-faced; her eyes appeared distant.

"What is going on?" the sheriff shouts.

"I don't know, but I hate snakes," says the border officer. Laurie looked at the officers and said firmly, "Now, you're going to let us go, and you are going to let us take the sheriff's truck, and you are not going to follow us, okay?"

"Yeah, yeah, sure," the sheriff said. By now, the other snakes were pestering the officers, biting them and wrapping all around them. "Just get these things off of us!"

"Come on, hurry up!" said Laurie.

"What in the hell was that?" Dizzy asks in confusion. "Did you learn some voodoo while in that hospital?"

"It's a long story," Laurie says.

"I told you," Cortés states. "You have been touched by the Gods."

"You sound like you are just touched, Enrique," Dizzy says in jest. Dizzy jumps behind the wheel, Laurie sits in the passenger seat, and Cortés hops in the back of the pickup. They speed off as the officers are still busy fighting off the snakes. Laurie immediately calls her buddy, James, to inform him to meet them at the Holiday Inn. But he was still a couple of hours away.

Chapter 10

Breaking News (1:30 pm)

On the outskirts of San Antonio, Texas, a seasoned journalist for *FOX 4 News (KDFW)*, Max Jensen, was dressed all dapper in his expensive suit. He was there doing a feature story. With him, was the cameraman and the pilot of the news helicopter that they took to get there. Max was at one time a rising star, winning all types of journalistic awards. However, his career had hit a cliff a few years earlier. After a bad cocaine habit, a sexual addiction, and a couple of sexual assault charges; Max was desperate and struggling to get back his once illustrious reputation as the best in the business. But even his boss was getting tired of his antics.

"I want to set up for the shot over here," Max said, pointing to a small empty field of grass. "Have the camera facing the

Prudential building, and be sure to get the building in the shot." His cameraman nods his head and begins to move the camera set up. A man in a suit on a cell phone walks by slowly. The man is loud and aminated.

"Billy," he says to the person on the phone. "My cousin just called and said there was some kind of standoff at the border between the U.S. and Venezuela." Max is reading his notes when he overhears the man. He stops and listens. "Yeah," he says, "they had their guns drawn and people were running everywhere in a panic."

"Excuse me," Max says to the gentleman, as he taps him on his shoulder. "Did you just say there was a standoff between U.S. Border Patrol and the Venezuelan army?"

"Yes, my cousin just told me."

"Would you mind doing a brief interview for FOX 4 News?" Max asks. The man gets all excited.

"Holy cow, you're Max Jensen! I'll call you back," he said to Billy. "I'm gonna be on the news with Max Jensen!"

"Jimmy, would you get a quick shot of

me talking to this gentleman?" Max asks the cameraman. "What's your name?" Max asks the man. Once Max finished the quick interview, he thanked the man. "Please sign this release form in order for us to put you on the T.V.," he requests of him. "Pack it up Jimmy," Max says to his cameraman. "We're heading to Laredo right now!"

"You're just gonna pack this up after all the work we've done on this story to head to Laredo cause some random guy gave you second-hand information?" Jimmy asks with concern and contempt.

"Jimmy, you don't get to be the top journalist in Texas by sitting on your hands," Max says confidently. "I can read people. That guy was not playing around. Now, we can sit here and let another station break the news or we can break it ourselves. Now pack it up, quick!"

"You've been doing this now for years, Max," says Jimmy. "You have gotten sloppy. You use to be a real pro with the best instincts I've ever seen. But you lost it in the bright lights somewhere, man. And your wife leaving you was the straw that broke your back."

"Hey, lay off the wife," Max says in anger. "I don't need a lecture right now, Jimmy. I'm telling you; this could be the big one; the one that gets me back to the top!"

"Yeah," Jimmy responds, "or the one that crushes you. That's your problem, man; you are all or nothing!"

"Is there any other way?" Max asks facetiously, as he pulls out his phone and walks away. "Hey, we are packing it up here," he states definitely.

"You got the story already?" his boss asks.

"No, I have something much, much better!" says Max.

"Much better?" the boss asks in anger. "Now Max, we are supposed to run the Banks story today and you don't even have the interview you went there for?"

"Listen, I'm gonna get you a story that you will get on your knees and kiss my feet for. Now just trust me!" Max says while gloating.

"You know what, Max," the boss announces. "You'd better, because if you don't, you'll be using those shoes to walk out the door and look for another job."

"Have I ever let you down, boss?" Max asks sarcastically. "Don't answer that! I'm taking the chopper to Laredo now; we'll be there in about an hour."

"Laredo?" the boss screams, as Max was hanging up the phone.

"Let's get a move on," Max says.

"You'd better be right about this one," Jimmy says to Max while carrying the gear to the chopper.

Stay Smart

Laurie, Dizzy, and Cortés arrived at the Holiday Inn in Laredo, Texas. James was still about an hour or so away. The group decided to rent a room and clean up and wait for him there. Dizzy checked in as the other two stayed out of sight. Once Dizzy paid and got the room key, he rendezvoused with the other two and they all headed to *room 112*. Being off of the streets and out of sight until James arrived was the only way for them to remain safe.

"I need to take a shower and clean up," Laurie announces, "but I need some clean clothes first. I'm gonna head to the gift shop and grab a few things."

"You sure that is a good idea?" asks Cortés.

"Burrito over here has a point," Dizzy declares. "They may be looking for you. You are the last person that should go."

"I didn't do anything wrong," Laurie proclaims persistently. "I was kidnapped and held against my will in the looney bin after my boyfriend and his friends were murdered by some freakish monster, and they lie and say I did it. I was chased by some lunatic Venezuelan general and had to sneak in my own God-damned country like some illegal immigrant, no offense Cortés. I've been pronounced dead, my name's been ruined, my business is probably closed for good, and I lost everything that I've worked for. I think I will roll the dice on this one!" Both men look at each other and nod their heads, conceding to her.

"I should go with you," Dizzy says.

"No," Laurie states adamantly. "I'm a big girl. After all I've been through, I think I can handle shopping at the Holiday Inn guest shop." Dizzy raises both hands halfway up, with his palms facing out, clearly yielding. Cortés turns and looked out the window. "I'll be right back," Laurie states firmly.

"Just be careful," Dizzy says with concern. "Here, take this," says Dizzy, as he hands her money for the clothes.

"Thanks!" Laurie utters, as she turns and closes the door behind her. It was the first time she had actually been alone and free in a long time. The gravity of the situation hit her almost as soon as the door closed. The fresh air and the sounds all around her seemed extremely amplified. Never before had she had such a heightened environmental sensitivity. The streets seemed abnormally noisy, almost debilitating. All at once, her brain was overloaded and overwhelmed by all of the aromas, odors, foul smells, and the smell of freshly cooked food in the air. She walked by a door that opened and closed just after she passed by.

BAM!

The closing of the door shook her momentarily. She turned and saw the woman who slammed the door shut. The man inside opened it. The woman began screaming at him. "You think you can treat me this way and I won't leave?" She put her hands over her ears. It was too much to bear or process. She took a deep breath. She reminded herself that she had been in situations like this many times before and that this was just a reaction to the trauma she had faced. Still, she shook from deep inside when any sort of overt stimuli stood out nearby. Finally, she reached the gift shop. As the door closed, so too did the perceived excessive overstimulation that occurred externally. Things quieted down. There was no one in the store except for her and the clerk behind the counter.

"Hello," the Mexican woman said to her as she entered, which triggered her anxiety slightly. Laurie just gave a half-hearted smile and walked toward the back of the store. She was able to focus completely now on her choices of clothing. Not that there was a large assortment of options, but she knew what she wanted based on the circumstances. She knew that she might be called on to run and hide at some point or even fight. Comfortability was the theme of this shopping spree.

She grabbed a white tee-shirt (that read: HOTEL, MOTEL, HOLIDAY INN), a pair of black, women's high waist stretchy yoga pants, and a pair of black women's running shoes with white souls. She also purchased a navy blue, zip-up hoodie (with the words: 'Holiday Inn' on it) to conceal her identity. She took the clothes up to the front and placed them on the countered at the register. The woman rang the clothes up one by one. With each article of clothing she scanned, she looked at Laurie funny, as if she recognized her. Laurie tried to keep her head down and not make eye contact. However, the woman was starring obsessively by now. The woman bagged the clothes and handed them to Laurie.

"How much?" Laurie asked.

"It's on the house," the woman said. Laurie slowly looked up and made eye contact with the woman.

"On the house?" she asked.

"We are all rooting for you!" the woman said as if she had seen her idol.

"Huh?" Laurie uttered.

"You are a hero around here," the

woman said. "You need to make it out of here and tell your story. This has been swept under the rug for far too long." Laurie didn't know what to make of the woman's comments. She gave a half-hearted smile and scurried out of the store with her belongings. As the fresh air hit her once again, she replayed that last interaction in her head. She was having a very hard time understanding what the people in the area were making her out to be, and if they were really on her side or not. In any case, her focus shifted to getting back to the room and showering.

Laurie walked through the door as if she was in a daze.

"Everything ok," asks Dizzy.

"Fine," said Laurie, as she bolted into the bathroom and locked the door.

"So, what's your story, Beaner?" Dizzy asks Cortés.

"My story?" Cortés asks humbly, as he wanted more clarification.

"Yeah," Dizzy said, "you know, your story...who the hell are you, and why are you here? And why are you such a big fan of Laurie?"

"I just want a life of true purpose," Cortés explains.

"Purpose?" Dizzy asks.

"Yes! Why are you here, Señor?" Cortés asks Dizzy.

"She is an American, we are American's," Dizzy states.

"That's it?" asks Cortés.

"What do you mean, that's it?" Dizzy asks, puzzled.

"Well, you Americans stand up for someone because they appear to be like you, in nationality or country. We here stand up for what is right and wrong. No color or nationality or country. People and morality should come first over self-interest."

"Well now, hold on a minute there, compadre," Dizzy says firmly, appearing a bit offended. "America is the greatest country in the world and Americans need to stick together."

"It's the greatest country in the world?" Cortés asks, rhetorically. "Have you taken a survey or just determined this on your own? Or is this just something you all just say, because your leaders say it?"

"What do you mean?" Dizzy asks. "Everyone knows this!"

"So, you assume this, not based on any admittance of any other country?" Cortés asks. Dizzy is confused by the question as if he never actually thought about it.

It was just something he regurgitated without giving it a second thought. "You say, America is the best country, as if you have taken a poll from other countries or won some mysterious contest," Cortés says poignantly. "You say 'God bless America, as if God has chosen you, and other countries are irrelevant. If you ask most of the world at this moment, they would tell you that the United States is a joke right now. But most countries are not rooting against you; we are actually rooting for you. And it just makes us sad that your country has so many ignorant, arrogant, entitled people that truly believe that you have the greatest country without any self-introspection or any true insight or true knowledge into other countries or cultures, other than what you are fed by the media; seems like a lack of nutrition to the rest of the world. A famous American, Edward T. Hall once said, 'every man sees something about you that you are incapable of seeing in yourself.' This is also true about groups and countries. It's like a man on your block walking down the street proclaiming every day that he is the greatest man on the block. Would you want to follow a person like that, even if he was?" Dizzy shakes his head, somewhat confused and embarrassed, even.

"Look, most countries want you to succeed. The United States Constitution is perhaps the greatest societal document ever written. But you didn't write it. To stand in front of another man and tell him you are superior to him because of what you inherited and what your ancestors accomplished will never get you respect in the world. You have to prove yourself in this life. And those who hide behind the accomplishments of others will always be seen as weak. You will be judged on what you accomplish, and your personal accomplishments alone."

"Well, I reckon, my little gordita," said Dizzy. "that was quite a speech. You ever think about running for office; in

Mexico, I mean?" Cortés smirks. "Listen," Dizzy says sincerely, "I have nothing but respect for all types of people. I moved here because I truly love the people and the culture. And I have been here several years, but I still have a lot to learn about the culture, and every culture, for that matter. And I completely understand where you are coming from; but if I don't get some grub soon, I'm gonna start lookin at you like you holdin the keys to the fridge. We can continue this chat later." Cortés laughs.

"Well, all you've been talking about is Tacos and gorditas," says Cortés, "sounds like you're in the mood for some Mexican food."

"Wow, Cortés, we've only known each other for a few hours and you know me so well," Dizzy responds.

Laurie comes out of the bathroom fully dressed and hits power on the TV remote.

"Well, look at you, little lady, looking all sexy," Dizzy says.

"Yeah, it's the new Holiday Inn clothing line," Laurie says sarcastically.

Coincidentally, the TV is on FOX 4

News. 'Breaking News,' flashes across the screen. The media commentator cuts the current segment short.

"Hey look," shouted Cortés, "it's the Gateway Bridge!" The three stopped and watched the broadcast.

"We have breaking news out of Laredo, Texas," the female TV Journalist recites. "Apparently, there has been an international incident at the U.S.-Mexican border involving an infamous United States citizen who has escaped from a Venezuelan mental hospital and has found her way to The U.S. Max Jensen is in Laredo, Texas. Max has single-handedly broken this story wide open. We are going live to Laredo, Texas now...Max, what can you tell us about this?"

"Well Jill, I'm standing here at the *Gateway to the Americas International Bridge*: the bridge that connects Mexico to Laredo, Texas over the *Rio Grande* river. Just a few hours ago there was a standoff here between U.S. Border Patrol officers and a crack team of Venezuelan military personnel, led by General Renier Rodriguez, Venezuela's top general. Now you may be asking, 'Why was the Venezuelan military at the Mexican/U.S. border?' Well, some eyewitnesses here told me that the standoff had to do with U.S. citizen, Laurie Orsted. Now, we all know Laurie from the confusing incident in Pavosa some weeks back, but we were all told that she was the perpetrator and the Venezuelan government claimed that she was killed due to an aggressive standoff with police.

Well, if she is in fact alive; this makes us question everything the Venezuelan government has claimed and would make sense why they were pursuing her so fervently. I spoke to several eyewitnesses at the Laredo border and they said the Venezuelan's were clearly hunting Laurie after what the General stated, and I quote 'escaped from a psychiatric facility in Venezuelan hours earlier.'

I spoke to one man, Carlos, who was enjoying the festivities around the Rio Grande here at the *Gateways to the Americas International Bridge* moments before the incident, and here's what he claimed!"

Carlos: "It was her for sure, Laurie. She bumped into me as she weaved her way through the crowd. I was caught off guard and I didn't think much about it until I saw the Chief come running up moments later and the tense standoff with border patrol. It was very close to ending in a firefight. In the chaos, Laurie got away."

"Was she with anyone else?" Max asked.

"I don't know," said Carlos. "I just saw her."

"And there you have it," said Max. "Other eyewitnesses claim a similar tale. We've attempted to validate the story, but as of now, no official has gotten back to us with an answer, which usually means they are trying to come up with a deflection story. And now the search for Laurie begins..."

"Well, I'll be," said Dizzy. "All this and they didn't even mention my name!"

"I wish they hadn't mentioned mine," said Laurie. "This is not good."

"Actually," Cortés objects, "this is a good thing. It will be easier to clear your name if they know you are still alive."

"True, but you need to stay out of custody long enough to tell your story," said Dizzy. "We don't even know if the U.S. might want this story to go away as well."

"Right now, I just need James to get here and get me somewhere safe," Laurie retorted. "They didn't mention you guys, so you don't need to worry yourself with helping me out any further."

"It's a matter of time before we get ID'ed," said Cortés.

"Yeah, ain't no point in splittin up now," Dizzy concurred with Cortés. "There's no way I could go back to my home in

Venezuela. The Chief would sniff me out like a dog looking for his bone. I am in this with you all the way," Dizzy affirmed.

"Me too," said Cortés. "I can help keep you safe. It will take them much longer to identify me than you too."

Chapter 11

Help Has Arrived – 3:00 pm

It was a long wait at the hotel. The tension grew as the moments went by, particularly for Laurie. Her eyes stayed fixed on the hotel door. Visions of police breaking through it danced in her head; so much so, that her subconscious was beginning to believe it was going to happen at any moment. Her heart rate was racing with the thoughts of going back to that psych-ward, or worse. She tried to calm herself and think of other things. But in reality, there haven't been any other things to think about for some time for her. Not since that harrowing night in Pavoso. Anything that happened before Pavoso seemed immaterial.

"Hey!" Dizzy called out, witnessing her staring at the door with an anxious look on her face. "Try to relax. Everything is going to be okay."

"I just wanna get out of here already," Laurie says. "It's not safe here for us."

"No one knows we're here, Mami," Cortés explains.

"Well, I know we're here," Laurie retorted. "And I'm sure we are in their search perimeter. Once we are a few miles away I will feel a bit better."

As soon as Laurie finishes her statement, her burner phone rings. She scrambles to answer, juggling the phone inadvertently and almost dropping it.

"Hello?" she said.

"I just pulled into the Holiday Inn parking lot," the man on the phone says. "What's your room number?"

"Don't worry about it," Laurie says firmly. "We're coming out now!" She hangs up the phone. "He's here!" she shouts. They grabbed what little belongings they had and rushed to the parking lot. Laurie was the first one out the door. The others raced to keep up.

"What kind of car does he have?" asks Dizzy.

"I forgot to ask," Laurie replies, as her

eyes scanned the lot fervently. "But I know he has an SUV. He bought it down here. I haven't seen him since he moved last year." Just then, a horn beep gains their attention. The SUV lowers its passenger-side window.

"Over here!" the driver calls out from his 2019 black Lincoln Navigator SUV. "Hurry up," he says, "cops are everywhere." Laurie hops in the front seat and the other two get in the back.

"Thank you so much for coming, James!" Laurie says with glee, as she leans over and gives the muscular, bald Black man a big hug. Once seated, Dizzy jolts in fear, as a big German Sheppard licks his ear from behind his seat. "What the hell?" Dizzy exclaims. "I haven't been kissed like that since the day I told my mama I was leaving home." The three others share a much-needed laugh.

"Bennett!" Laurie cries. The dog begins waging his tail and gets very excited. He even sounds as if he is crying, because he missed her so much. "Oh my God, I missed you boy," Laurie shouts. Laurie makes proper introductions as the SUV pulls out onto the street.

"How do you two know each other?" asks Dizzy.

"This lovely woman here saved my dog's life," James replies.

"I took care of Bennett after he got hit by a car," says Laurie. "And we became good friends after that."

"Yeah, and I was going through a messy divorce, and Laurie really helped me through it all. She is a great listener."

"Oh, I know a lot about divorce," said Dizzy. "My ex-wife could start a fight in an empty house." James laughs.

"You know what they say Dizzy," says James. "As a man, you have two choices in marriage. You can either be right or be happy."

"Yeah," Dizzy says. "Love is grand, but divorce is a hundred grand." James and Cortés start cracking up.

"Oh boy," Laurie says, "you guys are gonna get along just fine. So where are we headed, James? I remember you saying something about a friend of yours."

"Well, I met this big-time Oxford University Professor a couple of weeks ago at some fancy dinner party," James reveals.

"It was for a political reason; to discuss political strategies for a mayoral candidate that we both know. Anyway, the happenings in Pavoso—and I'm so sorry about Harry and the others, Laurie (Laurie nods in thanks but wants to hear more)— so, naturally that topic comes up, as it does everywhere, and I say you and I were great friends. I teared up a bit, as I thought you were gone. So, this guy says that he is an anthropologist who majored in *Aztec Cultural Studies.* He said that he read a lot about the case because there were rumors online that an ancient Aztec spellbook was recovered."

"Yes," Laurie said. "It's a long story, but I found it in the basement of the house we were staying at."

"Oh wow, then he is definitely going to want to meet you now!" says James. "He also said that he read up on this Whistling Man tale, and he found that it is in relation to an ancient Aztec curse. So, he said he would have wanted to meet you if the circumstances were different (you being alive, that is), and that he would have likely been able to help you with the knowledge he has. I called him on the way to pick you up and he said he would drop everything and to bring you by his house, and that he would keep us safe. But then he called back fifteen minutes later and his energy changed dramatically. He sounded urgent. He said that he just spoke to Cardinal Abramo from Rome! This Cardinal guy is like one or two levels under the Pope and may be Pope one day, even. Anyway, he happens to be at *St. Mary's Church in Fredericksburg*, and he kept saying how this thing was bigger than we think and to please meet them at the church."

"Can we trust this guy?" Dizzy asks cautiously.

"I don't see why not," James replies. "He has no need for money or notoriety or any affiliation with those after you. Plus, what are our other options?" The group had no answer for that. They were skeptical, but beggars can't be choosers. At least they might get some answers, they thought.

"It's a little more than a three-hour drive, so just try and relax. You guys have been through a lot."

"I guess it's worth a shot," Laurie

says. "And they don't even know the half of the story I'm about to tell them!"

Wake the Dead – 6:55 pm

A priest sits in a leather chair in the "study" (as it's called in this particular establishment) of a coffee house in the city of San Marcos, Texas. He is wearing a black clergy shirt with a white tab collar under his black robe with the hood down, and black pants. He looks a bit agitated and nervous as he takes frequent small sips from his large hot coffee. His hands shaking, making waves in the coffee; some tipping over the edge and spilling on the floor. He looks at his watch, takes a large swig of his coffee, and stands to his feet. He throws the coffee cup—which is a little less than half full—in the trash and proceeds to the front door.

"Take care Father Hennessey," the young male counter clerk shouts.

"See you soon, my son," the priest says, not bothering to look in his direction. The priest opens the door, pauses, and then looks around briefly. He throws his hood over his head and continues out the door.

Overhead, the sign reads, *Wake the Dead Coffee House.* He walks down Old Ranch Road with his head down. Darkness has recently consumed the area. The priest can't help but feel like he is being watched. 'I'm probably just being paranoid,' he thinks to himself. After all, he always has extreme feelings of guilt and anxiety on *pickup day.* A few paces later he turns into a small, dark alleyway and continues walking. Out of the shadows, a figure appears abruptly. The priest flinches and jumps back.

"Don't scare me like that," the priest says firmly, as he removes the hood from his head. The man smirks. "Are we good?"

"Always," the man says. "I have your usual." The priest hands him money and in return, the man hands him a small plastic bag filled with tiny crystallized solid white rocks, better known as crack cocaine.

"See ya next time," the dealer says and walks away. The priest pays his goodbye no mind. For once the dealer had handed him the bag, it was as if the dealer had disappeared. His focus was on one thing. Out of his pocket, the priest pulled a Pyrex pipe. He had made a filter earlier out of six small brass screens, rolling them into a burrito-type shape and stuffing them into the pipe as not to burn his mouth or throat. He opened the bag and put a small portion of its contents into the pipe. His lighter is a cigar torch lighter, which has a wind-resistant flame. He lights it and holds it to the edge of the pipe for a moment, then vacillates it side to side a few times. The heat placed directly on the drug causes a crackling sound. The hollow pipe fills with smoke. The priest inhales.

"*Zoot!*"

The smoke inside the pipe vanishes. He holds it in for a second or two, then exhales. Immediately, his demeanor changes. The expressions of anxiety he wore so noticeably on his face just moments earlier have now disappeared like the smoke he has just exhaled. He zones out for a moment until he hears what sounds like a bottle being kicked along the concrete back down the alley where he had entered. He quickly puts the pipe behind his back.

"Who's there?" he shouts. But there was no answer. His fear of being seen was trumped by his desire for another hit. He reaches into the bag again; this time in haste, and packs the pipe. He speedily takes a few more hits before stuffing the pipe, bag, and lighter into his pocket. He throws his hood back over his head and walks through the alley in the opposite direction he had come, as he always did. This wasn't exactly the quickest way back to the church, but it was the one with much less traffic. Again, however, he hears that bottle skimming along the concrete in the distance. He turns but again sees nothing, as it is pitch black. A second or two later, he hears a *popping sound*; the sound of a bottle breaking on the ground, sounding as though someone had thrown it with great force.

The priest picks up his pace a bit, making a right turn onto Owens Street. The church is only about a seven-minute walk from there. But he feels strange like someone is watching him. He can't shake the feeling. Just then he hears a loud whistling-scream that shakes him to his core. It sounds far away, but devilish and terrifying nonetheless. He turns and sees a hooded figure standing in the alley entrance where he had just exited only moments earlier. The figure's face is not visible, but it does appear to be looking directly at him. As the priest begins to walk, the figure walks in step, in the same direction. The priest starts getting worried. Being high on crack didn't help. He begins walking faster. However, the figure, like a shadow, matches his exact pace. The priest turns his head toward the fast-approaching figure.

"Who are you?" the priest shouts, not breaking stride. "What do you want?" The priest is now terrified and he breaks into a full sprint. After a minute, he turns, but the hooded figure is gone, vanished. He stops and looks around curiously and in bewilderment. The streets are empty. There isn't a person in sight. The silence is deafening. He turns back around in the direction he was headed, and to his horrifying surprise, *The Whistling Man* is standing right in front of him, arm's length away. Father Hennessey freezes, and his face rapidly drains of all color. The figure pulls back his hood, exposing his grotesque face. He lets out an aggressive roar right in the priest's face. The breeze and stench from the roar rush over the priest's face like high winds blowing over a mountain, which makes him flinch. Father Hennessey's facial expression unexpectedly goes from shock and terror to an expressionless, comatose-like appearance.

Chapter 12

Hells Bells – 7:00 pm

"Laurie! Laurie! Wake up!" the faint voice said, sounding almost like a distorted, distant shout; a slow-motion echo down a long hallway. "Laurie!" This time, the shout was heard a bit clearer. Laurie twitches rapidly as her eyes open abruptly. She sees a parking lot, the back of a church, and hears church bells ringing. "We're here," the same voice (James) informs her. The sun had just recently faded, and the group was now walking toward the back entrance of the church under the cover of darkness.

Just before the group reaches the short staircase leading to the back entrance, the back doors swing open.

"James!" the man says excitedly.

"Professor Clayton," James responds, as the two shake hands.

"And you must be Laurie?" the professor asks.

"Hello," Laurie says cautiously.

"I've read so much about you," says the professor. "I'm Dr. Robert Clayton, Professor of Anthropology at Oxford University. You can call me whatever you'd like. Most people call me *'Professor.'* We have much to discuss. But first, please come in and get settled." The group walks in and follows the professor into the first floor of the church. As they enter, each dabs their right hand into the holy water and performs the sign of the cross. Dizzy is the last to enter. He looks at the holy water, dreading the ritual. He dips only a tiny bit of his right index finger into the water. As he does so, he closes his eyes, and his face tightens and wrinkles. He is bracing himself for a lightning strike. When none comes, he gains confidence and performs the sign of the cross. As he does so, the bells ring, which jolts him slightly, thinking the bells are signifying his entrance as sacrilegious. He looks around for a moment and then realizes it was just a coincidence.

The large church is a majestic sight to behold. The aesthetic beauty is palpable and overwhelms the senses. The lighting is magnificent. The detail in the architecture and color schemes provide the onlooker with a feeling of ebullience. As the group absorbs the aesthetic beauty of the designs, they notice a priest kneeling at the altar praying.

"That is Cardinal Francisco Abramo," the professor reveals. "He is part of the *Council of Cardinal Advisors*, picked specifically by the Pope to serve as an advisor. Serendipitously, he happened to be in town because something big is going on that actually involves you," the professor relays to Laurie.

"Me?" Laurie asks in a confused voice. The professor nods his head matter-of-factly.

"I will let him explain," the professor says. Cardinal Abramo opens his eyes, looks up, and sees the group walking toward him. He slowly makes his way to his feet; his knees cracking and his back aching, as he slowly rises to his feet. Laurie takes the lead, walking a bit faster than the others. She grabs the Cardinal's arm and helps him to his feet.

"Cardinal Abramo," she says respectfully, "it is a pleasure to meet you."

"Laurie Orsted," he says resolutely," the pleasure is all mine." The two shake hands. "We have been waiting for you and for this day for many years," the Cardinal professes.

"For me?" she asks in confusion.

"Follow me, we don't have much time," he asserts. The Cardinal led the group toward the back-right of the church, leading to a door. Beyond that door is a narrow hallway that leads to an elevator. The Cardinal shuffled through the many keys on his large-ring keychain until he found the right key. The group waited in anticipation. Only the sound of dangling keys can be heard. He put the key in and turned it to the right, summoning the elevator from the lower floors. The large, two-door elevator opened, and fit the entire group comfortably. Once inside, Laurie noticed that there were no buttons representing floor numbers, only three keyholes, placed vertically on the panel. The Cardinal put a different key into the middle keyhole and, again, turned it to the right. The elevator quickly proceeded downward.

The elevator doors opened after a brief ride. "This way," the Cardinal said, as he made a right down the corridor. After a few steps, he stopped at a large antique double wooden door with a medieval look to it and standing about twelve feet high. The doors opened and led to a large study room, with thousands of books neatly tucked away on bookshelves. The room had a large antique desk, several antique leather couches and chairs, and an old white, gray-haired gentleman wearing a suit and white gloves who served as the butler.

"Make yourselves comfortable," the Cardinal says. "Would anyone like a drink?"

"I'm probably gonna need a whole

bottle of that holy water ya'll make here, your preciousness, cause I haven't been in a church in a while," Dizzy blurts out. The Cardinal smiles.

"Don't mind him, Cardinal, he is not housetrained just yet," Laurie says, as she gives Dizzy a dirty look.

"Oh, it's quite alright, dear," the Cardinal says. "I've heard the pilot was a bit of a character." Dizzy looked surprised when the Cardinal knew he was a pilot.

"I would love a drink, Mr. Cardinal," Cortés said politely. The butler went around to each of them and asked them what they wanted. Dizzy and Cortés both got whiskey on the rocks. The professor ordered a brandy, neat. Laurie and James both asked for water. Dizzy walked around with his drink looking at the various books and paintings. Cortés sat quietly observing what was to come next.

"So, Professor Clayton tells me you had a run-in with the beast down in Pavoso," the Cardinal says to Laurie. "I'm sorry about your friends. Do you have any idea why you survived and they did not?"

"Luck, I guess," Laurie outwardly

postulates.

"Not quite," he retorts. "Do you believe in fate, Laurie? Destiny?"

"I don't know what I believe in anymore after the things I've seen recently," she laments. "But something very strange has been happening ever since I entered Pavoso." Dizzy had an open book in his hand when he shouted out, "My mother use to say, 'A man often meets his destiny on the road he took to avoid it.'"

"Ah, your mother was a wise woman," says the Cardinal. "Did anything strange happen, Laurie, while you were confronted by the monster? Anything that seemed out of the ordinary?"

"A lot of things," Laurie states. "It felt as though something was directing me; like something was seeing through my eyes at times and making decisions for me."

"Can you remember the exact moment when things changed in this regard for you, Laurie?" asks the professor.

"Yes!" Laurie states unequivocally. The Cardinal and the professor lean in.

"When?" the Cardinal asks curiously.

"Sarah and I were in the basement of

the home we were staying at when we found a book."

"What kind of book?" The professor asks.

"It was some sort of ancient Aztec spellbook." The Cardinal looks at the professor and nods his head as if he had already known, they've already discussed this, and that this gave them confirmation.

"I don't mean to be rude, guys, but can you possibly give us a hint as to what's going on here?" asks James. "Laurie has been through too much lately to be anyone's guinea pig."

"That is what we are here to find out, James," says the professor. The Cardinal signals to the butler to dim the lights.

"Would you all gather around here please?" the Cardinal asks. "I need complete silence during this demonstration, please. Not a sound from anyone." The Cardinal grabs a big cross and a small bottle of holy water. "Close your eyes and clear your mind," he tells Laurie. "Try to remain as still as possible." The Cardinal begins dousing Laurie with small doses of holy water. As he does so, he begins speaking.

"Spirit, reveal yourself in the name of the Lord. Come forward and speak to me." With every few words, he douses her with holy water. Suddenly, Laurie's eyes open and are focused on the ceiling. No blinking, just wide-eyed and in a trance-like state.

"State your name to us," the Cardinal declares. But Laurie remains silent and fixated on the ceiling. "Who are you?" the Cardinal demands. "State your name!" Laurie's eyes slowly move from the ceiling to the Cardinal. She looks directly at him. "Who are you?" he asks again. This time, however, Laurie speaks, but in a deep voice that is not compatible with her own.

"I am Toci, the earth Goddess," she reveals. "I am the mother of the Gods."

"Why are you here?" the Cardinal asks. "Why are you inhabiting this woman's body?"

"She is the chosen one. She has been chosen to combat the evil forces that are currently assembling; chosen to fight Mictlantecuhtil," the spirit discloses. "I entered her during a ritual she conducted with the sacred book."

"Mictlantecuhtil?" the Cardinal asks.

"Is he coming?"

"He is already here," she informs him. "*The Lord of Death* is here, and he will raise an army of the dead that will consume the planet and destroy and enslave humans."

"Where is he now?" the Cardinal asks.

"He is close. And he and his army will be ready on the birthday of our Lord."

"Can you stop him?" he asks.

"Yes, but I will need an army of well-trained Soldiers. And not just in combat, but in spirituality. Once Mictlantecuhtil is defeated, his entire army will fall back to hell with him." Laurie's body begins shaking and her eyelids blink furiously. Her body suddenly goes limp, and she falls on the couch, unconscious.

The Rub

Laurie awakens in a haze. All four men are standing above her riddled with anxiety. She sits up. James holds a bottle of water to her lips and tilts it while gently leaning her head back, giving her a few sips.

"What the hell happened?" she asks.

"Do you remember anything?" asks the professor.

"Not after the first few blasts of holy water. I was transported to a swimming pool with my mother when I was young."

"It is believed that you are possessed by the great Aztec Goddess, Toci," the Cardinal announces to her.

"Who?" asks James.

"Toci is known in Aztec mythology as the 'mother of the Gods,'" the professor states.

"Oh yes," Laurie proclaims emphatically, "That's what the spell was; I remember that. But I didn't think it was real!"

"Toci is an earth goddess associated with fertility, warfare, curses, and the patron of the midwives," explains the professor. "Toci is frequently depicted wearing a headdress with cotton spools and a skirt of snakes."

"That's the woman who comes to me in my dreams!" Laurie exclaims.

"Toci is also linked to healing and recognized for her ability to cure ailments," the professor continues. "You might have heard the phrase, 'Old wives' tale,' about curing colds and sicknesses?" Everyone node their heads up and down. "Well, that's attributed to Toci, although it has been said that she can also cure people from certain fatalities as well."

"So, you're telling me that I am possessed by a goddess?" Laurie asks in shock.

"Not a goddess," said the professor, "THEE goddess!"

"Well, I'll be a monkey's uncle," says Dizzy.

"I knew it!" shouted Cortés, as he performs the sign of the cross and looks up.

"Then what the hell is that other thing out there killing people and taking their bones?" asks Dizzy.

"Great question, Dizzy," the Cardinal says.

"There is an old Venezuelan urban legend about a boy who killed his parents and was banished into the woods," said the professor.

"Yeah, yeah, *El Silbón, what about it?*" *Dizzy asks.*

"Well, apparently while his

grandfather, the old Aztec man, Zuma, was putting the curse on him, he messed up. He chanted the wrong curse," the professor states.

"Didn't the guy know what he was doing?" James asks.

"Yes," said the Cardinal, "but when dealing with the supernatural, they are cunning. They have many ways and means of tricking humans. Not only that, but Zuma probably hadn't chanted a curse or spell in some time. He likely misspoke or simply chanted the wrong spell. Under the circumstance—having just learned that his son had been butchered by his grandson—I'm sure his emotional state was erratic at best. He may have left the book in the basement and chanted the curse from memory, just chanting the wrong one."

"So, what did he turn El Silbón into?" Dizzy asks.

"Mictlantecihuatl," says the professor.

"The who to the what now?" asks Dizzy in confusion.

"Mictlantecihuatl," the professor repeats. "The Lord of Death."

"Oh great!" James shouts. "The Lord of Death!"

"According to Aztec Cosmology, there are thirteen Celestial levels and nine Underworld levels. The souls of the dead must pass through each lower level until they reach Mictlan—known to many as Hell—where the death God rules over."

"Wait, wait, wait," says James. "So, you're telling us that the creature we are talking about, and the one that killed Laurie's friends is—"

"Satan, himself," the Cardinal confirms. The room immediately filled with gasps of anxiety and sighs.

"In Aztec mythology," says the professor, "Mictlantecihuatl is portrayed as an open-mouthed monster who devours the souls of the dead. He is sometimes portrayed as an owl, and crows follow him around and obey him."

"What is he doing here?" Cortés asks. Dizzy looks at Cortés and whispers, "Good question."

"We are not one-hundred percent sure," the professor says. "But we believe he is here to conquer earth."

"Oh, great!" Laurie says sarcastically.

"But," the Cardinal says firmly, "I have these." The Cardinal grabs two long, yellow poster-sized papers that are rolled up tightly and tied with a red ribbon, and in a round plastic casing. "These are secret scrolls that have been housed at the Vatican in Rome for centuries. They are written in Sanskrit, and Professor Clayton translated them as best he could earlier."

"You know how to read Sanskrit?" Dizzy asks. "You must not have had much of a childhood, man."

"The first scroll explains and prophesizes the beginning of the story, the one we just discussed. The second scroll, however, says that (the professor opens the scroll and begins reading), 'In tlen matlakse hora, or 'At the eleventh hour,' the beast will summon the crows to retrieve the bones of his victims, and they will meet at the designated spot where the ritual will take place."

"What ritual?" Laurie asks.

"Something that will bring upon the apocalypse," says the Cardinal.

"And," the professor continues, "they

will meet at the 'Koyoktli miktlampa,' or the 'Gateway to Hell,' where the ritual will be performed. Ostensibly, the result of the ritual will be opening the gate between earth and hell, whereby the demons in hell will be unleashed as well as what it calls 'the game-changer,' if you will (the translation is a bit spotty for that one) and 'the most treacherous of all creatures,' the '*Tlayouateyaochiuanimeh.*'"

"What in the world is that?" Dizzy asks.

"*The Shadow Warriors,*" the professor says with trepidation.

"The what?" James asks.

"We don't know exactly," the Cardinal says. "I did read in some other classified documents about shadow demons that float and have no real earthly substantial form, but I haven't been able to cross-reference yet, because we just found this out, and it appears we don't have much time before this occurs."

"When is this supposed to happen?" Cortés asks.

"We translate the eleventh hour to mean one of the final acts before the apocalypse begins," explains the Cardinal. "The demons will bring diseases on the world like we have never seen before, starting with a biological one soon after the gates open that will change the world as we know it now. They will divide and conquer. Brother will be against brother, etc. The antichrist will be at his most powerful. And the downfall will take place quickly. We must stop the beast before these rituals are carried out or we will likely be at a great disadvantage."

"And the kicker here," says the Professor, "is they need a priest to conduct the ritual."

"That's cold!" says James.

"And, it must be conducted on the recognized birthday of Jesus Christ."

"That's north-pole on steroids cold!" Dizzy says.

"What does this have to do with me?" Laurie asks.

"You, my dear," says the Cardinal, "are the only one who can stop him!"

"I'm the only one who can stop the devil from carrying out the apocalypse?" Laurie asks, shocked.

"Yes!" says the Cardinal.

"Heavy!" Cortés says.

"There must be a mistake!" Laurie shouts in fear. "I never asked for this!"

"This is your destiny, Laurie," the Cardinal says resolutely. "You are the chosen one."

"The chosen one?" she says in anger and confusion. "I can't even balance my checkbook half the time."

"God chooses those who are pure of heart, righteous, and ready."

"I'm none of those things! I just tried cocaine for the first time. How do I get her out of me?" Laurie asked frantically. "I don't want anything inside of me! I don't want any of this!"

"That's the tricky part," the Cardinal says.

"Yeah, they call this part 'the rub,'" said the professor. "You need her in you. We need her in you; humanity needs her in you."

Suddenly Laurie's eyes roll to the back, she wabbles a bit and then passes out on the couch again. Everything just goes black.

Chapter 13

Devil Within (11:40 pm - December 24, 2019)

Destiny City Church (San Marcos, TX), midnight mass is about to start. Only minutes remaining until midnight mass, which is the most crowded mass of the year. Many of the mass participants start noticing that Father Hennessey is acting strange and erratic, more than usual. It wasn't just the routine crack cocaine this time. Not that they had any idea about that. It was the fact that his demeanor had changed from normally a bit strange to dark and distant. However, he remained focused, which wasn't normally part of his character. He is typically known for stumbling around topics during sermons, expecting others to bail him out. Typically, incoherent. However, this time, he told everyone that he would do this one on his own, which confused them all.

Twenty minutes before the service started, Father Hennessey approaches his most loyal church staff members, those being three top-level church committee members (two women and one man). He asks them to step outside with him for an urgent, private discussion. They walk to the back door of the church. Each of the three is a bit taken back by the sudden change in routine and demeanor of the priest. Nonetheless, they were not expecting what was about to transpire. As the priest swung open the door, he held it for the other three to go outside. A figure was standing with his back facing them, hoodie on his head, and hands spread out like Jesus on the cross, with his head facing toward the sky.

"I want you all to meet someone very, very special," Father Hennessey said in a dark voice. The three stood waiting for the figure to turn around. Instead, he let out a breath, which blew black smoke into the air. The smoke lingered for a second or two. The church committee members stared in awe and confusion. Then, it broke off into three separate clouds. All three continually changed shape until they developed eyes and mouths with menacing fangs. Simultaneously, they each picked a subject and raced toward them. By the time the three had a chance to react, the smokey shadows had entered them and taken control of them. Their faces turned expressionless.

Midnight Mass (December 25, 2019)

With everyone in their seats, the church choir begins singing, acapella, the song, '*O Come, All Ye Faithful.*' Twenty-two Alter boys lead the procession, all walking up the nave toward the altar in pairs of two; each holding long polls with lit candles on top that stand several feet above their heads. They pass the crossing and, just before they reach the two stairs leading to the chancel, each of the two altar boys split;

one goes right two steps, the other goes left two steps. Then they turn and face the chancel, again, and continue toward the altar, where they line up just in front of, each new member lining up away from the center.

The associate pastor, Father Thompson, follows close behind, holding a gold-plated Bible high above his head with both hands. He parades it around the stage, showing all the altar boys, and then the crowd, who are still singing along with great enthusiasm. Father Hennessey steps onto the chancel and heads for the pulpit. Father Thompson lays the book down on the pulpit just before Father Hennessey reaches it. The well-timed orchestration ends with Father Hennessey at the pulpit just as the music and signing halt. Silence, for just a few seconds. Then, Father Hennessey speaks.

"Ladies and gentleman, welcome to this historic midnight mass celebration. I want to break from the norm just a bit this evening and talk to you, not about the death of him [he points up], but about what got us here and what is needed to get us to the future. There is only one word that comes to mind: 'sacrifice.' [Many in the crowd say "Amen"]. In the Bible, John 15:13 says, 'There is no greater love than to lay one's own life down for a friend.' No greater love! Mark 10:45 says, 'the son of man did not come to be served, but to serve, and give his life for the ransom of many.' [crowd begins to cheer and a crescendo builds]. Ya see now, that word 'ransom.' That means we are being held hostage. And, unless WE, PERSONALLY, sacrifice our lives; WE will never be free. [crowd cheers loudly].

Ya know, in the United States Justice System, people are considered innocent until proven guilty. That means they get their day in court. They get to tell their side of the story.

There are always at least two sides to a story, not just one! Could you imagine someone put you in jail and they say he did horrible things and he never got a chance to tell his side of the story? You would assume he did those things. He would be guilty in the court of public opinion. They would call for his head. Now imagine that person silenced was your mother, father, brother, sister, significant other, or child. Wouldn't you want to hear their version of events? ['Yes,' the crowd yells]. So why are we always talking about Jesus only? Jesus said this and Jesus did that and Jesus walked on this, Jesus, Jesus, Jesus. What about the testimony of the other side? [the crowd gives a collective 'huh,' showing confusion, not sure where this is headed.] (*Father pauses*).

Well, I just wanna say, thank you! Thank you for your

sacrifice here today. [crowd applauds lightly]. If not for you, and your sacrifice here today, the true destiny of this planet would never come to pass. Today, my good friends, our mantra will never be truer: {crowd chants along with Father Hennessey} 'For we are no longer chasing dreams. We are fulfilling destinies.'"

Father Hennessey steps away from the podium and raises his hands high. The crowd starts cheering. The band was confused because Father Hennessey went off script from what was rehearsed. So, they improvised and started playing music as a transition into what was supposed to be the next segment. As people rejoice to the music, Father Hennessey looks at his three top-level members and gives a dubious head nod, which signals for them to covertly step outside the church. Each of the three is situated by one of the only three exits from the church; the side doors, on opposite sides of the chancel, and the large front doors. Father Hennessey uses the confusion to step offstage and quietly departures through the right-side exit (if facing the altar). As he did so, his male confidant locked the door behind him from the outside. Seconds later, the two female confidants meet them there, with Father Thompson as a captive.

Father Thompson has a bruise on his head and his hands are tied behind his back.

"What are you doing?" Father Thompson cries. "Have you gone mad?"

"Have you secured the other two exits?" Father Hennessey asks them.

"Yes," says the first.

"It is done," says the second. The beast walks up quietly. They all look at him.

"Has the gasoline been distributed properly around the outside of the church?" Father Hennessey asks. They all say, "Yes," in unison. The beast then raises his right hand, makes a fist with his thumb erect, and runs his hand across his neck, simulating cut the throat, like the WWE character, The Undertaker. Each of the three committee members heads to their respective entrances and lights them on fire. Father Hennessey and the beast stand in front of the church; the beast restraining Father Thompson.

The flames began to burn at each exit and quickly turns into a raging fire. The music is still playing inside. The band looks around in confusion, not sure when to stop, as the practiced routine had been altered. They did, however, stop and wait for a hopeful signal from Father Hennessey that the next phase of the service would continue without a hitch. After a few seconds of silence, however, the people inside start smelling smoke. They look around at each other to get a perspective on the situation. Yet, no one has any clue that their condition was becoming more volatile and perilous by the second. It only takes one church patron to scream,

"FIRE!"

to cause mass hysteria. By now, however, the fire had begun to blaze all along the perimeter of the church. People began running toward each exit, only to realize that the doors have been locked. People closest to each of the exits began shouting that the doors are locked. Word traveled quickly to everyone else inside the now burning coffin. Panic ensued. Some patrons broke through the stained glass windows and jumped, only to be engulfed in flames. Others tried desperately to break through the doors. Some searched for buckets of water to hold off the flames; while some sat in tears praying.

The Whistling Man and his new associates stand outside, watching the flames overwhelm the church. The beast is reveling at this moment, as he had waited for this for so long. Father Hennessey, who was miraculously gifted with the new ability to speak fluent in the Nahuatl language, at the subliminal direction of the beast, began chanting a ritual sacrificial spell.

"Inin tlamanalistli ka given nik in teotl iuimikistli, mictlantecihuatl, as se gift iuikpa tlalli. Iuelilisuanse nikan ka unlimited, iuan ignite in apocalypse."

("This sacrifice is given to the God of death, Mictlantecihuatl, as a gift from earth. May his powers here be unlimited, and ignite the apocalypse.").

"Please stop this!" Father Thompson screams. "Open the doors! Let these people out!" The horrific screams from the hundreds of people inside the church rang out into the night. Those who had come to celebrate the birth of the Lord Jesus Christ were now in the throes of a menacing crime, the likes of which have never been seen. A ritual that will help bring about the apocalypse. Entire families, with their children at their sides, are burning to death and dying of smoke inhalation slowly and agonizingly. Smoke fills the church to the point that visibility becomes nil.

Once they realized the job had been completed, the beast and his recruits turn and walked away, as the steeple collapses into the church. The screams are heard no more; only the crackling sounds of flames and heavy wooden structures burning and crashing down on themselves. The police and fire engines come racing to the scene with sirens blaring. The media follows close behind the police cars and fire engines.

Unphased by all the commotion and new arrivals, the beast and his twisted group casually waltz down the street. They slip into a dark, woodsy area, unnoticed, and are soon out of sight; just as chaos takes over outside the church.

Chapter 14

The Powers Within (12:30 am - December 25, 2019)

Laurie is walking slowly in a large field with a vast mountain array in front of her. Just a couple of hundreds of yards away, she sees nothing. She turns and sees thousands of armed troops in blue uniforms behind her, and several women in nun outfits with guns as well. Suddenly, the sound of a thousand Aztec death whistles can be heard from just over the mountain ridge. Seconds later, a distant rumbling gets louder and louder, as a charging army becomes visible coming over the mountain. She squints, but cannot see the approaching figures clearly. But all of a sudden, she does, seeing an aggressive beast-like army charging, with strange shadows flying overhead of them. Unexpectedly, she falls to the ground, with The Whistling Man straddling her, roaring in her face with his big canine teeth just before she tersely awakes.

Laurie sites up swiftly and defensively on the couch and looks around. She sees a woman in a tight nun's outfit sitting behind the desk. It looks like the nun who was directly behind her in the dream.

"Good, you're finally awake," the nun says.

"I just saw you in my dream," Laurie states.

"Laurie," the Cardinal says, "this is *Ezmisa*. She is a Combat Nun and head of *The Sectarians*, a secret army of the church. She will brief you and help you with your training."

"Training?" Laurie asks in a dim voice.

"Get up," Ezmisa commands. "We have a lot of work to do!" Ezmisa uses her cell phone to make a call. "She is awake. Let's get started."

****

Moments later Laurie, Professor Clayton, Ezmisa, and the next two Combat nuns in rank behind Ezmisa (Edmina and Edwina) all reach the training facility, which is one level down (the bottom level). James, Dizzy, and Cortés remain upstairs. The nuns appear stylish and combat-ready. They are all dressed in the same gear: A wet look mini dress with a sheer fishnet chest and upper sleeves, a full front zipper closure, a white-collar chest piece, a cross detail bodice, finger loop long sleeves, a nun habit headpiece, and black leather pants with matching wet-look.

The training facility is very large, with many different training tools and weapons. The underground structure, in general, is a sight to behold. There is a training facility the size of four high school gymnasiums. There are two food stores, a drug store, two clothing stores, an underground train, and a roadway for cars and trucks that both lead to a variety of different underground tunnels and facilities.

"We believe that you have many different powers," the professor explains.

"And we need to not only find out but help you learn how to harness and control them," Ezmisa clarifies.

"What kind of powers?" Laurie asks.

"Let's start with moving an object without physically touching it," Ezmisa suggests.

"You mean with my mind?" Laurie asks while tittering.

"Look," Ezmisa says angrily, "I don't care much for you and I'm not very happy about having to teach an undisciplined, unspiritual person how to lead us; so how about you make this easy for us all and just listen, okay?"

"Isn't this God's will and he chose me?" Laurie asks.

"Yes, that is correct," says Ezmisa.

"So, if you're doing God's work and not happy about it, maybe you're the one who needs an attitude adjustment." Ezmisa takes an aggressive step forward toward Laurie, and Laurie mirrors her. Professor Clayton steps in between them.

"Ladies, ladies!" he shouts. "We are

on the same side here. And we have a fierce enemy who will destroy us all if we cannot come together right now. Time is limited. So, are we going to do this or not?" Each woman stairs the other down for a moment, but realizes that the professor is right. They turn and walk away to compose themselves before coming together again.

"Okay," Laurie says, "I will take this more seriously and give this a shot." Just then, the Cardinal walks in and feels the tension.

"Is everything okay in here?" the Cardinal asks.

"It's fine, Cardinal," says the professor. "We are on the first exercise, your excellency."

"Laurie, look at me," the Cardinal commands, as he moves closer to her. Ezmisa steps away. "Here I have a rock." He holds it up, and then bends down and places it on the ground. The rock is about 5 inches wide, 4 inches tall, and 3 inches deep, weighing about 2-and-a-half pounds, and it's flat on the bottom. "I want you to move it with your mind."

Laurie puts her right hand out and

focuses, almost trying to move it with her hand. She strains and strains, but the rock will not budge. "No, no," the Cardinal objects. "You don't need your hands. You just need your mind. Forget the physical for a moment and just feel the energy all around you. Let the energy field lead your eyes right to the rock and through it." Again, Laurie focuses. This time her hands are at her sides. She strains and strains again, but still no movement. But then something strange happens. Small yellow rings form a direct path from her eyes to the rock. They are spinning slowly, and time seems to slow a bit for Laurie. Her focus is razor-sharp like it's only her and the rock. The Cardinal speaks, but it seems to her that he is speaking in slow motion. His lips are moving slowly, but it's muffled, distorted audio.

The rock shakes a bit. Just enough that everyone can see it shake, but it didn't move. Laurie continues trying. The strain dissipates into a smooth natural feeling, a comfort, like greased wheels turning. She is locked in.

Zoom!

The rock shoots across the floor. It must have slid a clear ten yards. She lets go. Things around her immediately go back to real-time.

"Holy shit!" she screams. The others look at her with wide eyes, shocked. The Cardinal looks surprised at her response. "Sorry, I mean, holy cow! I mean, wow"

"You did it!" the Cardinal says with excitement.

"Beginner's luck," Ezmisa says under her breath to Edmina. Everyone appeared to be excited about the accomplishment except Ezmisa.

After a few more tries, Laurie was mind-tossing that rock all over the place. She started to hit targets that she aimed for in dead-center.

"Okay," the Cardinal says, "now we are going try something a little harder." Edwina walks in carrying a box, holding it from underneath with both hands. Very carefully, she carries it and sits it down on the ground in front of Laurie. When Laurie gets a look inside the box, she sees a sick, dying *Northern Mockingbird* lying on his side. His faint chirps brought out the emotions of sister Edwina, who shed tears and had to look away. She looked at Edmina, who acknowledges her empathetically will a look. She then looks at Ezmisa, who rolls her eyes apathetically.

"I need you to heal this bird, Laurie," the Cardinal says.

"Cardinal," Laurie says with apprehension, "I'm not a God."

"You are not," he agrees, "but you have a deity within you who is speaking through you. Just give it a try. I don't know the exact proximity you need to be, but try it without actually touching the bird, as you did with the rock." Laurie leans in. She puts her right hand out this time, palm facing the bird. "Focus, Laurie," the Cardinal encourages. After a few seconds of intense focusing, the yellow rings appear again. Laurie doesn't know the words to say or what to do. In her mind, she asks the divine power in her to heal this bird. She visions the bird standing on his feet and looking healthy. Suddenly she hears a voice say, "help me, please." She jumps back and looks around in confusion.

"Did you say something?" she asks

Ezmisa?

"No," she responds, with a puzzled and annoyed look on her face.

"What did you hear?" Edmina asks.

"Someone clearly said, 'Help me, please.'"

"It may have been the bird," says the professor. "Toci was known to have animal telepathy. It was one of her most known and admired traits. And I'm guessing, that since Laurie works with animals and has an innate ability to connect with them, that this ability is very strong in her."

"Oh my," speaks the Cardinal. "Try to talk to him again."

"I must heal him first," she says. Laurie reaches out again and focuses with all of her empathy. Within seconds the bird springs to his feet and flies into the air. Everyone gasps and starts clapping, except for Ezmisa. Yet, even she is amazed, just not showing it outwardly. The bird lands on Laurie's shoulder. It leans in toward her ear.

"Thank you, your highness," the bird says to her. The others only hear chirping.

"He spoke to me again!" she exclaims. "He said thank you, your highness! How is this possible?"

"It appears that you have inherited the ability to manipulate the electromagnetic waves to stimulate their olfactory receptor neurons," says the professor, "allowing you to send an impulse to the brain's olfactory system."

"Is there an English translation to that?" Laurie asks sarcastically.

"Yes," the professor explains, "you can talk to animals."

"There are many more things you need to learn and continue mastering through practice," the Cardinal says, "but one other main function is the ability to summon Toci at will. You need to work with Toci. You both need to bond and trust each other. You need to trust that when she is in control that she will do what is needed. When summoned, she can increase your strength, awareness, and abilities dramatically but only momentarily."

"Correct," said the professor. "You need a symbiotic relationship with her. She is in you and working with her and understanding her will only increase performance."

Mano a Mano

"The most important way this will be useful is during combat," the Cardinal says. "Ezmisa," the Cardinal calls out, signaling her to step in.

"Now this is gonna be fun," Ezmisa says with a devilish grin.

"What, you want me to fight her?" Laurie asks. The Cardinal nods his head. "But she is like a man." Ezmisa has a bamboo kendo stick in her hands. She charges Laurie and hits her once in the left knee, sending her right knee to the ground. The next shot hits Laurie in her neck. Laurie leans forward on all fours. The final strike is to the middle of her back, sending Laurie face down on the mat. All this occurred in a few seconds. Ezmisa is fast, with good technique, and efficient with every strike.

"What the hell was that?" Laurie shouts. Ezmisa smiles, as the professor winced.

"That was me kicking your you-know-what," Ezmisa replies with a smirk.

"Again!" shouts the Cardinal. "Laurie, do as you did with the rock. It's similar, but this rock is moving toward you." Ezmisa got into the ready position. Laurie got into an awkward fighting stance. She looked out of her element. Ezmisa charged forward. Suddenly, time slowed. Ezmisa's blinding speed was now reduced to the speed of a turtle.

Ezmisa swings for Laurie's head. Laurie moves out of the way easily. It even shocks her. Ezmisa's eyes and follow-through are looking at the ground in front of her while Laurie stands almost directly behind her. Ezmisa turns and looks at Laurie in anger. She regroups and attacks again. This time, Ezmisa swings for Laurie's left knee again. Laurie moves it effortlessly as if she anticipated the strike. Ezmisa immediately sends the stick in a stabbing motion toward Laurie's torso. Laurie side steps the stick and stares at it as it is still moving forward.

"Good, good, Laurie," the Cardinal says. "Now try to strike back."

Ezmisa is now furious. She swings the stick at Laurie's head with all of her might.

Laurie grabs the stick effortlessly as it's coming down on her, rips it out of Ezmisa's hand, and tosses it on the ground. Ezmisa lets out a brash scream and charges Laurie. As she is running full speed, she lowers her head, in an attempt to tackle Laurie at her mid-section.

Laurie again, easily side-steps her, sending Ezmisa flying to the ground. She quickly gets up and turns around. Laurie closes her eyes, but she can still see Ezmisa's aura or the outline of her and all her movements. Again, the yellow circles appear between her and Ezmisa. Time slows down again. Ezmisa begins charging in slow motion. Laurie takes a deep breath and jolts her hands forward as she exhales forcefully.

Zoom!

Ezmisa shoots backward, off of her feet and to the ground, as if the force of a 200-mph wind had just struck her directly. Edmina and Edwina both chuckle softly. Edwina gathers herself and looks at her fellow nuns snickering. She gives them a dirty look. They both attempt to wipe the smiles from their faces quickly. Yet, their lips have a hard time holding back a quiver.

"You did it, Laurie!" the Cardinal shouted with joy.

Just then, one of the regular nuns comes running into the facility with an urgent message.

"You all need to come quickly!" she shouts in terror. "Something terrible has happened!"

Panic Button

The entire group follows the nun into the restaurant area next door, which has multiple TVs.

"What is it, Tiffy," Ezmisa asks.

"It's horrible, just horrible," Tiffy responds in a tearful voice. "You must see for yourself." Tiffy leads them to the first TV by the bar, where the clergyman bartender is waiting with a remote in hand and a somber look on his face. The national cable news station is on the screen. The clergyman turns the volume up loudly on the remote.

[TV news anchor in the studio] "Breaking news...A mysterious fire has burned down *Destiny City Church in San Marcos, TX.* We don't have all of the details, but sources are saying that the doors were allegedly locked from the outside, trapping hundreds of church-goers inside as fire engulfed the church. Max Jensen is live outside of the church. Max, what's going on over there? What happened?"

"Well, Donnie, this is a sad, sad day in the United States, and the world, for that matter! This church that you see behind me, or what's left of it, was filled with hundreds of church patrons, according to my sources. They were locked inside the church, from the outside. Allegedly, gasoline was poured all over the outside of the church. Police say it was a deliberate and well-orchestrated act. Police do not know, or will not say, who they believe carried out this heinous act, but they did say that they are currently labeling this a hate crime. That's all they would say.

However, an eerie 911 call released by police just minutes ago suggests that the head priest, Father Hennessey, and three other Church members were involved in the heinous attack. Now, this is unprecedented, that police would reveal such a call so soon.

However, they say it may shed light on the situation and help bring the killer or killers to justice sooner than later. They say they have other 911 calls corroborating the following information. Let's take a listen. And please be warned, this audio is allegedly from a victim who died inside this church only about an hour ago, and it's not for the faint of heart."

Operator: 911, how can we help you?
Church Goer: Please help! We are

stuck inside Destiny City Church in San Marcos, TX! All three doors are locked and the church is on fire in every direction! We don't have much time! *[screams]*

Operator: Is there any other way to exit the church?

Church Goer: No, no...someone locked all the doors from the outside! *[screams]*

Operator: How many people are lock in the church with you?

Church Goer: Hundreds of people! [screams]

Operator: Do you know who did this?

Church Goer: I believe it was Father Hennessey, the head pastor. He gave a very strange sermon about sacrifice.

And he and three others are nowhere to be found. This was planned. We are being sacrificed. Please help us. *[screams]*

Operator: Stay calm, please; help is on the way.

Church Goer: We're not gonna make it! It's too late! *[Call disconnects]*

[Horrifying female screams]

"Oh my God, this is awful!" shouts Edwina, with tears in her eyes.

"It was them; I know it!" yells Cardinal Abramo. Suddenly, Laurie's eyes appeared to roll to the back of her head. Only the whites of her eyes were showing. Ezmisa took a step toward Laurie as if she was going to help her. The Cardinal reached out with his right hand and put it in front of Ezmisa's mid-section, stopping her from proceeding.

Laurie's thoughts were being thrown at her in pieces. They were flashing before her eyes in tiny snippets, evanescent, like a series of short *graphics interchange formats* (GIFs). She saw a dark cemetery. She saw a wild-eyed priest. She saw a scared priest whose hands were being restrained by rope. She saw a bright red ring in the ground and a raging fire. She saw one priest slit another priest's throat. And finally, she saw the beast; and eerily, their eyes met; he looked as if he saw her during the vision! The beast screamed and grabbed her. She shook loose and her eyes quickly rolled back into view of her friends. She shook her head slightly intending to readjusting her eyesight and balance.

"I know where they're going," Laurie said in a matter-of-fact voice.

"Where?" asks the Cardinal.

"San Marcos Cemetery," Laurie relays. "And we gotta hurry!"

"It's about an hour-and-a-half drive from here," the Cardinal describes. "But if we take the underground railway, we can be there in about forty minutes!"

Chapter 15

Dawn of the Dead (1:15 am – Christmas Day)

The beast had set up an altar in a predesignated area at the *San Marcos Cemetery*. In front of them was a large hole in the ground, in the shape of a ring, that's diameter is approximately one mile. The hole is deep. It looks as though it had formed fairly recently. A light smokey mist is emanating from the hole. The male figure pushes Father Thompson from behind toward the altar. He stumbles forward.

Caw, Caw!

A dozen crows come flying in from high above. Somehow, they have managed to work together to retrieve and carry the beast's sack of bones that he had stashed in the house in Mexico. Most of the crows play a hand in carrying the bloody sack. They gently drop it in front of the altar and begin circling it from high above.

"Please, don't do this!" Father Thompson begs Father Hennessey. But he pays him no mind. The two females begin to disrobe until they are naked. The beast rips off all his clothing and gets naked as well. His eyes glowing with a blue-colored light. He has no eyeballs to speak of. His veiny, rotting exterior and odd-shaped head, with its extra-long forehead, is a terrifying, gruesome sight. The beast grabs Father Thompson with his right hand, picks him up off the ground by the back of his robe, and slams him back first onto the make-shift altar. He puts his face close to Father Thomson, who is terrified, and opens his mouth and lets out a large roar. The upper half of his gums show about one-two inches from lip to teeth. However, it's doubtful that Father Thomson saw anything but the large canine teeth of the beast.

To subdue him, the beast backhanded Father Thomson so hard that he knocked him unconscious. The beast was able to speak to Father Hennessey telepathically. He did so, letting him know it was time to begin the ceremony. The two naked females stood beside the altar, one on each side. Father Hennessey began by saying the Lord's prayer backward in Latin.

****

The underground railway was quite the sight to behold. The train was some futuristic model, something of which had not yet seen by the general public. There were no wheels. The train hovered above the tracks by some mysterious, secretive new magnetic technological breakthrough. The interior is luxurious, fit for a king, or more fittingly, a Pope or Cardinal. The interior of this sleek, aerodynamic, magnificent machine is more reminiscent of a luxury penthouse apartment rather than a train. It holds comfortable sofas with cushions and soft furnishings, airy glass modules fitted with computer screens, a well-stocked bar, and a double-decker observation deck (which is being manned by several armed male *Sectarian Soldiers*). It also has a lounge area by the bar and private pods. Riders barely feel like they're moving, even though the train runs at much higher speeds than any train known to man.

Laurie, the Cardinal, and the three Combat Nuns were all aboard the train (along with several *Sectarian Soldiers*). The rest had been ordered to stay behind.

"Why didn't the others come with us?" Laurie asks.

"It's safer for them to stay behind," the Cardinal retorts.

"We could not afford to have the beast possess them and turn them against us," Ezmisa explains. Her tone was always combative. Her face, always appearing angry.

"What exactly are we stepping into?" Laurie asks.

"According to our intel," Edmina says, "we believe that the burning of the church ritual readied a hole in the cemetery for a final ritual."

"The final ritual is most likely taking place there now," said Edwina.

"A ritual for what?" Laurie asks.

"To open up the gateway," Edwina says.

"Gateway to what?" Laurie asks inquisitively.

"The Gateway to hell!" Ezmisa announces grimly. Laurie just stares, expressionless, as she is in deep thought. She is just trying to absorb this information. Things are happening so fast. She had just learned not long ago that she can move objects with her mind. Yet, she didn't even have time to process or celebrate her newfound talent before learning this new information.

"I don't know if I'm ready for this," Laurie says with trepidation.

"I know you need more training," the Cardinal agrees, "but unfortunately time has not permitted so. We are at a great disadvantage. We must pray that the Lord will guide us and that destiny will ultimately be on our side, as it has been written."

"But I can't do this," Laurie says. "Moving rocks is one thing. Fighting Satan? Are you kidding me?"

"Look," Ezmisa shouts firmly. "You are more powerful than all of us combined. Do you think that I like saying that? I have spent my whole life training and studying. I have sacrificed everything for God and my religion. Do you think that I am happy that someone like *you* (said sarcastically) gets such power bestowed upon her and is virtually a heathen and has done nothing to earn it?"

"Well, I didn't ask for this, and I don't need this shit!" Laurie screams. "And I definitely don't need some bitchy, jealous nun with her panties in a bunch because Jesus is just not that into her, talking down to me all the time." Ezmisa is deeply offended and stands up. Laurie stands as well.

"You want me to toss you around again like I did back there?" Laurie asks cynically.

"Go ahead and try!" Ezmisa says menacingly, as the two need to be separated by the other two nuns.

"Ladies, ladies!" the Cardinal shouts in a deep voice. They both stop.

"You know what," Laurie cautions, "okay, let's do this. He did kill my man and my friends and almost killed me. If Satan wants some, then he can come get some!"

"Oh, now you're John Cena?" Ezmisa says sarcastically.

"And when this is over, I'm coming for you next, *sister*." Laurie says condescendingly.

****

Father Thomson is in the midst of completing the final stages of the final ritual that will open up the gates of hell and bring Satan's army, *The Whistling Man's army*, to earth in its physical form.

"*Et animarum obscura sunt in porta, pulso!*" (Translation: "The dark souls are at the door, knocking*!*").

"*Dominus mortis, hoc tibi do supremum sacrificium. Adveniat regnum tuum, fiat illud ad ianuam aperire. Et consumat habitatores terræ, adveniat regnum tuum, fiat.*" (Translation: "Lord of death, to you I give this final sacrifice. Let it open the door to your kingdom. And let your kingdom consume the earth.")

The male figure hands Father Hennessey a knife. He raises it up and begins talking in tongues. The beast is walking backward, most steps look unnatural.

Father Hennessey stops chanting and brings the knife down. Pure evil radiates through his facial expression, as he looks at his victim. Father Thomson awakens and appears a bit disheveled. Father Hennessey approaches. Father Thomson realizes what is happening and tries to sit on the table. The male figure grabs his head and pulls him back down, holding him in place. Father Hennessey holds the knife to the right side of his throat.

"No! Don't do it!" Father Thomson screams. "Lord, into your hands I commend my spirit!" In one quick motion, Father Hennessey slits his throat from right to left, almost ear to ear. Blood gushed from the incised area. Father Thomson chokes and gasps furiously, while blood spills from his neck and mouth. The two naked females each hold a wooden bowl. They collect the blood as it spills off of the altar that has been designed much like a sewer drainage system, funneling the blood toward the bowls. Father Thompson takes one last desperate gasp before his body goes limp.

One female pours the blood from her bowl into the other bowl. The beast walks over, grabs the bowl and holds it up high. He then drinks the blood, chugging it like it was a sweet, tasty drink.

There is silence for a few moments. Then, the smokey mist from the hole clears, as if a vacuum had just sucked it up. A distant rumbling sound can be heard. Ominous, but faint, aggressive screams sound-off. Deep, quickly approaching, growls grow louder and louder.

Just then, one dark claw digs into the top of the hole right near the altar. It appears to struggle, like a baby being born. More and more of it emerges until its face can be seen. Its eyes glowing with a red luminescent glow. The demon makes his way upward and, in a few seconds, his ten-toes are standing near the altar. He bows to the beast. The beast casually and slowly nods his head forward. The first demon through is *Asmodeus*, third in command behind Satan.

Seconds later a small fly flies out of the center of the hole. It is making an inordinate sound, not buzzing like a fly, more like a loud electric cord. Everyone watches as it flies upon Father Hennessey's left shoulder and sits. Feeling uncomfortable, Father Hennessey slaps his left shoulder with his right hand, crushing the fly. It falls to the ground by his feet. The beast cringes then flares up with anger. The fly lies there for a second, appearing dead. However, in an instant, it changes form into a full-sized demon, sizably bigger than Asmodeus. It lies there in the fetal position for a second or two. Then, however, it rises, awkwardly, with its feet, legs, waist, and arms contorting. It stands on the palms of its hands and its feet, with its stomach facing the sky. It walks on all fours away from Father Hennessey, but then back toward him. Still, in the same position, the creature raises up hands and head first, and in a second is towering above Father Hennessey, standing nine-foot tale.

It is the demon *Beelzebub*, second in command to Satan. He is the general of Satan's army and the most vicious demon. Even Satan wouldn't want an equal fight with him. He is Satan's muscle. He is fully committed to Satan's cause; the highest-level member in the cult of cults. Father Hennessey freezes in fear.

"I'm so sorry!" he says. "I did not know or mean to harm or offend you." Beelzebub turns and looks at *The Whistling Man* and smiles. He is the only demon that can speak.

"I'm happy to be back and in your presence, Lord," he says, in a deep, raspy voice in surround sound. He then turns back to Father Hennessey.

"You, hurt me?" He says and lets out a menacing laugh. Beelzebub smiles at him and summons him to the edge of the ring. "Look, they are all coming," he tells him. "All because of you. We owe you a debt of gratitude that cannot be repaid."

"Oh, oh, it was my pleasure, Lord," Father says while shaking in his shoes.

"Enjoy this," Beelzebub says. "You have earned this moment!" Father Hennessey smiles and relaxes a bit. Evil growls grow louder and louder from inside the hole. Looking down the black hole, Father Hennessey can hear the growls like they are very close, but he cannot see anything yet in the darkness. Suddenly,

Beelzebub sticks his right claw through the back of Father Hennessey. He does it so violently and aggressively that most of his palm is protruding out of the stomach of the priest. Beelzebub lifts him up, showing his strength as he holds him there for a second, and then flings him like a rag doll into and down the hole. Beelzebub turns to *The Whistling Man* and says, "He will be my personal pet when I return." *The Whistling Man* lets off what seems like laughter. At that moment, the growling and grunting became unbearable. Moments later, a plethora of demons come crawling out of the hole. Some are crawling on top of each other to escape into this new world and be reunited with their king.

Outnumbered

Laurie, the Cardinal, the three Combat nuns, and twenty *Sectarian Soldiers* exit the train near the cemetery. They rush over to the cemetery but are too late. High up on a hill, behind the bushes they hid, watching covertly, as they get there just in time to witness the killing of Father

Hennessey. After that, an onslaught of demon Soldiers rise-up from the ground. The group watched in awe and terror. It was no longer their place to stop this incident. The best they could do is gain as much intel as possible. They witnessed more and more demons coming through the ring. They had not anticipated the astronomical numbers that would be coming onto this planet. It was shaping up to be the fiercest army ever assembled. That was before the *Shadow Warriors* appeared. Shadowy pitch-black figures with no legs or feet come flying quickly out of the hole, maneuvering like jet fighters.

"How can we fight This?" Ezmisa asks.

"I thought you had faith?" Laurie asks sarcastically. Ezmisa doesn't even appear to acknowledge Laurie's insulting sarcasm, as she is transfixed with the ongoing raid of the earth. Yet, still, Ezmisa can't let that comment pass.

"I've never been one to believe that faith and reason are polar opposites," she replies.

"Okay," Laurie says, "So, I bet you a thousand dollars we're fucked."

"I don't gamble," Ezmisa says.

"Oh, so you don't have faith?" Laurie asks.

"You know what," Ezmisa retorts. "I will take that bet, cause it's a bad bet on your part."

"What do you mean?" Laurie asks.

"Well, if you win, you are dead. And if you lose, you owe a thousand dollars. And I thought you were smart." Ezmisa chuckles condescendingly.

"Okay," Laurie says, "I guess it's me that has no faith. And I will gladly pay you a thousand dollars if we get out of this alive."

"You can make a check out to the church," Ezmisa says, with a smirk on her face.

"What the fuck are those things?" Laurie cries regarding the shadows.

"Oh my God!" Edmina says. "this is not good!"

"They are the Shadow Warriors, mentioned in the secret scrolls," the Cardinal explains, who looks visibly shaken. All the color has drained from his face.

Asmodeus grabs the bloody bag of bones and walks over to the hole. He tosses it in. Moments later, a large black cloud rises from the hole and floats toward The Whistling Man. It surrounds him, and then he consumes it. Suddenly, he rises; his feet leave the ground. The bones have made him more powerful and have given him greater abilities. One is the ability to hover in the air.

Just then, the Aztec death whistle sounds, far away. Laurie looks up and locks eyes with *The Whistling Man*, same as they did in the church back in Pavoso. The creature is floating twenty feet above the ground. They both pause for a second and hold the stare. Then, the creature summons his followers to attack!

"Oh shit!" Laurie screams in terror. "Run!!!"

To be continued...

"The Whistling Man III" coming in 2022...

Also, be sure to check out Will's new horror novel "Nomed Station." You'll never look at a train ride the same way again! On sale May 2021!

Please visit:

https://willsavive.com/

Facebook:

https://www.facebook.com/dawhistlingman